Grimly Emily uncovered Colleen and touched her daughter's leg. She lifted it, flexing it at the hip and knee, then shifted the pressure, attempting to push the leg downward. Colleen moaned and fought, trying to keep her knee pulled up instead of letting it relax and stretch out on the bed.

"I was afraid of that," Emily whispered numbly. Her child was lying here in a hospital bed with almost certain meningitis, and no one was doing anything. They were all involved with other cases, thinking Colleen could wait. But she *couldn't* wait! A child could die from meningitis. At the very least, she could be badly damaged. Emily felt a sudden, unreasoning, white-hot anger. Her daughter was suffering, and no one cared!

"Someone said there was an emergency here?"

Emily's head snapped up. No! she thought dazedly. Of all the doctors she didn't want to see, she especially didn't want to see Dr. O'Shea, followed immediately by Dr. Shelby.

"Oh, it's you, Greer. What are you doing, ignoring your patients upstairs to take care of some kid in Emergency? Isn't that frowned upon by your supervisor?"

Emily bit her lip to keep from screaming at the man. She loathed him, but she needed him. Colleen needed him. . . .

Other books in the R.N. series

R.N.²

FEVER PITCH

Patricia Larkin

LYNX BOOKS
New York

RN #2: FEVER PITCH

ISBN: 1-55802-060-8

First Printing/December 1988

This book is published by Lynx Books, a division of Lynx Communications, Inc., 41 Madison Avenue, New York, New York, 10010. The name "Lynx" together with the logotype consisting of a stylized head of a lynx is a trademark of Lynx Communications, Inc.

Printed in the United States of America

0 9 8 7 6 5 4 3 2 1

FEVER PITCH

Chapter One

Emily Greer looked up from the charts and sniffed. There was a very definite smell of cigarette smoke in the air. Smoking was strictly forbidden in the rooms, and she knew that the solarium was deserted—she'd just taken a break and walked down through the darkened corridors to the glassed-in observatory.

For the past few weeks, the hospital had been filled with patients who were night walkers, and it was refreshing to see that finally they'd all gone home and there weren't any patients in the lounge. The moonlit night was magnificent, and the windows in the solarium were opened just enough to catch the tangy, fresh smell of an awakening spring. Emily leaned forward, drinking in the wonderful scent, her head resting briefly against the icy metal of the window frame. It was enough to make her want to burn her winter uniforms. She longed for the freedom of crisp, lightweight cotton. No more coats, she thought, sighing.

No more heavy boots, and the eternal sweaters, and worrying about the wind-chill factor.

She was ready for spring, all right!

As she moved away from the window, the smell of smoke became more pronounced, and Emily frowned.

If the smoke wasn't coming from the solarium, then it had to be one of the patients. But who on earth would be foolish enough to light a cigarette in his or her room? There was a good reason for the prohibition against smoking—there were volatile gases, bedding, and other equipment that could burst into flame at the slightest provocation. Suddenly she had a sneaking suspicion who it might be, and hurried out of the solarium into the hall.

"Emily, do you smell that?" Nancy Ann Richards looked up from the record she was annotating.

"Cigarette smoke?"

"You smell it, too?"

"Sure do!" They nodded and raced in opposite directions, hoping to catch the patient who was smoking and snuff out the cigarette before someone complained, or worse, before there was a disaster caused by the patient's disregard of hospital rules.

Emily ran down the hallway, the thick soles of her white shoes making a dull, thudding noise that most of the patients wouldn't even hear.

"Don't let it be Martin Harper, okay, God? I'd appreciate it . . .," she whispered through gritted teeth. She was angry enough with the man anyway, since she'd drawn baby-sitting duty tonight for the fifty-five-year-old spoiled brat.

Good old Martin Harper—he'd been a royal pain in the backside since Dr. O'Shea had admitted him for tests and possible surgery. Harper was a mess.

2

He'd smoked so long and so hard that his lungs had lost all the elasticity they'd ever had. The man was anemic, he had clubbed fingers from oxygen deprivation, and he preferred smoking to eating. He waited for the nurses to serve a meal, then left his food sitting while he removed the oxygen from his nose, climbed out of bed, wrapped his old brown robe around him, and shuffled out to the solarium where smoking was permitted, where he would wheeze away another five minutes of his life while his lungs worked overtime to try and compensate for the lack of oxygen. His face was pudgy and swollen from the effects of continuous asthma medications, and his hands trembled constantly as a result of other drugs poured into his system to keep his airways at least partially open. Still he smoked.

Dr. O'Shea had lectured, pleaded, and ordered, but nothing had made even a minor dent in Harper's conviction that he had every right to smoke wherever he happened to be. In disgust, Dr. O'Shea had turned the whole police action over to the nurses. He expected them to watch the man like a hawk, even though each of them had at least six to eight other patients to care for. They couldn't take the time to check on Mr. Harper every other minute.

Emily caught the edge of the doorway, and swung into Harper's room. She slid to a stop by the door.

The smoke surrounded the bed, thick and stifling. It had the same acrid quality she had noticed with other nonstop smokers, as if their lungs had been permanently permeated with the smell of smoke, and there was nothing left of the normal human scent when they exhaled, even if they didn't happen to be smoking at the time.

"Mr. Harper, stop! Don't move, don't take another puff on that cigarette!" Emily wanted to run away, to escape from the horrible possibility of flames and explosion that could erupt at any second. Fire panicked her. Ever since she and her first husband had been caught in a burning car, she hadn't been able to cope with the thought of fire.

Emily peered at the man's form through the fumes. He was still hooked up to the apparatus that fed oxygen from the outlet in the wall through clear green tubing and through the cannula that fitted into his nose and sent the oxygen down his airways.

Mr. Harper looked at her and then puffed again on his cigarette. The green nosepiece was almost obscured by wreaths of smoke, and she saw the red glint of the cigarette as he took one last deep drag before she could snatch it away from him. The hiss of the oxygen was clear—and deadly.

"Oh, God . . . " she breathed again, but this time in pure panic, "please, not fire . . ."

She tried to calm her nerves and think of a way to get the cigarette out of the man's hands without starting a conflagration. She heard Nancy's rapid footsteps approaching. "Nancy, it's in here!" Emily called to the other nurse. "It's Mr. Harper!"

If that cigarette ignited the oxygen . . .

If there was a flash fire . . .

The thought had barely entered her head when an invisible hand seemed to pick her up and throw her against the wall. The room was bathed in an intense golden glow. The same hand that had knocked her down picked up Mr. Harper and threw him toward the end of the bed. A sheet of flame outlined Mr. Harper as he flapped through the air, the hospital gown burning its outline into his flesh. He landed in a heap at the end of the bed, his legs and arms flung at odd doll-like angles. The ring of hair around his scalp flared and burned. Emily could see Mr. Harper's

4

mouth opening as he screamed, but she could hear nothing but the deadly roar of the flames.

Emily reached toward the outlet in the wall for the oxygen, but there was no way that she could move toward the fire. The wall belched a steady gout of fire as oxygen fed through the silver spigot, turning the system into a very effective flamethrower. The blazing gas roared across the room. Anything in the way of the flames melted, twisted, and then vanished—first the blankets and pillows, then the plastic bag that had been connected to the intravenous drip machine. The machine itself was momentarily wrapped in flames. It beeped madly for a few seconds, then uttered one mournful note and died. The flames rose even higher, obscuring the bed and racing up the drapes.

Emily couldn't breathe. She was virtually paralyzed by fear. She had to get out! . . . If only she could take a breath and make her legs work so she could crawl out of here! But first she had to turn off the oxygen.

There was a second explosion and she heard glass shattering. A rumbling shook her and rattled her teeth. Her arms ached, and she was getting dizzy. The force of the air that was being siphoned from other rooms and out the window made the whole room vibrate. Drapes flared, carrying the flames in long billows.

The intense heat began to dissolve the plastic covering of the mattress and ignite the stuffing. The old brown robe was gone in the flames, as were the flowers by Mr. Harper's head and the mystery novel he had been reading the last time Emily had looked in on him.

"Let me out of here . . . ," Emily prayed, but no one was listening to her. She could feel the heat of the flames on her skin, singeing her eyebrows and the

hair on her forearms. She wondered for a moment whether her eyebrows would grow back again. . . . Wouldn't it be funny if they didn't? Her thoughts started on a mad merry-go-round that told her she was on the verge of going into shock.

Emily finally shook off her terror long enough to move. Dropping flat on the floor, she pulled herself toward the door, aiming for the outline of light in the intense darkness caused by the smoke that roiled through the room and out the windows.

She had to get out! She had escaped a fire before and she could do it again.

In the distance she could hear the soft-toned alarm bell ringing, alerting the staff to a disaster.

She had to reach the oxygen cut-off. But where was the valve? Try as she might, she couldn't form a coherent image of where the oxygen ring was. Down the hallway? Just outside the door? She didn't know.

From the speakers in the corridors, she heard the calm, even voice of the operator announcing a call for "Mr. Red" on Ridge Six East. Only other hospital personnel would know that "Mr. Red" was the code name for fire, and that a real disaster was under way on the sixth floor.

"Close the fire doors!" Denise Frazier's voice cut through the rising hysteria from patients who had been alerted to the danger by the explosion and the sound of splintering glass. "Get the patients out—hurry!"

"What happened?" Denise hurried into the room through the swirling smoke, and pulled Emily off the floor. She was shocked by Emily's appearance—a huge bruise was already forming under her right eye where she had hit something that hadn't yielded during the explosion. Emily's right forearm was cut. Denise guessed that a piece of glass had sliced through the skin. There were no visible burns on Emily's skin, only the flaking that showed that most of the hair on her arms had been singed by the intense heat.

Emily's eyes were wide with fright.

"Mr. Harper . . . ," she gasped.

"How did that man get a cigarette? Is he still alive?"

Emily shook her head dazedly. She didn't know if he was or not. With the explosion and the blowtorch effect, she doubted it. But the questions calmed her and gave her time to focus on what needed to be done. Her terror was subsiding, and she could hear the patients who needed help in getting moved away from the fire calling to the nurses.

Only thirty seconds had passed since the explosion, but time had taken on a different meaning. The seconds seemed stretched into hours. She had to help save the other patients, get the fire reported and a team on the floor to contain it.

Emily shook herself. She was going to be all right. It wasn't an automobile accident, it was a hospital fire. Mr. Harper had caused an explosion by smoking around oxygen. If she didn't turn off the oxygen, the whole building could go up.

"You help Nancy and Keith. I'll take care of the oxygen," Emily said to Denise. Now she remembered where the shut-off was.

"Good girl," Denise said as she ran from the room.

Emily dashed past the head nurse and ran for the wall opposite the nurses' desk. The fire had been raging for a full minute.

She grabbed the d-ring and began to turn, hearing the almost subliminal hiss gradually die away, until there was nothing more in the tubes. The roaring from Mr. Harper's room faded as the fuel was withdrawn, but the drapes still smoldered, and the mattress was nothing but a cinder. Black smoke still rolled out of the room.

Water. Emily looked up in surprise. There was water pouring over her, cold water washing her burned skin and uniform and making her injured arm instantly ache. The sprinklers had kicked in, set off by the smoke from Mr. Harper's room. The brass heads sprayed water into every corner of the corridor, drenching nurses and patients alike, and wetting every piece of paper and chart at the nurses' station.

"Out of the way!"

The in-house fire response team barreled through the fire doors and down the hall.

"This way—follow me!" Emily gave the d-ring a final twist and then ran down the hallway toward Mr. Harper's room.

"There are still flames in the wall, and around the window—there's a man in there, I don't know if he's still alive," she cried, as the men raced into the room, playing their firehoses against the flames that were still eating at the wallboard and framing. Within a matter of seconds, they had extinguished the last of the flames. Smoke continued to pour from the mattress and the melted plastic equipment in the room.

Emily moved in right behind the men as they controlled the fire. "Damn fool!" she whispered under her breath, her concern for the patient overwhelmed by rage at the havoc his thoughtlessness had caused.

Then she looked down at the bed, and almost retched. Mr. Harper was breathing—she could see the movement of his chest. But there wasn't a patch of skin anywhere on his body that wasn't burned. His face was red and swollen, and it was only by sheer chance that he had any eyelids left. He was completely devoid of hair. She could see the marks on his arms and across his stomach where the gown had rested as it burned. There were areas where she could clearly see the muscles below the surface of the skin. The gray, flaking wounds gave off the smell of badly roasted meat.

"Code team here, stat!" She screamed the order, and heard the affirmative response from one of the other nurses on the floor. She leaned forward, reaching automatically for the mask and oxygen valve set in the wall, then dropped her hands. She couldn't start the oxygen again to keep the airways open. There was no oxygen available because the idiot had blown the apparatus out of the wall and flambéed himself at the same time.

She watched helplessly as Mr. Harper struggled to breathe. She could do nothing for him—he was too badly injured for her even to attempt anything. If he lived, the emergency team would take care of intubation before they moved him.

Suddenly she remembered something that one of the doctors had told her—if someone has been badly burned, douse the patient with water. It could make the difference between life and death in some cases. There were sprinklers operating in the room, but they were not completely dousing Mr. Harper.

Emily turned to one of the firemen. "Get a hose over here and help me wet this man down," she ordered.

"Wet him down? He's not still on fire, is he?" one of the men asked in surprise.

"Do it *now*! Give me a gentle spray. We've got to keep him wet until the team can get here," Emily shouted.

"Everything under control here?" Keith Jennings, one of the few male nurses at Ridge Hospital, looked in the doorway on his way to escort one of the ambulatory patients out of the smoky corridor.

"It'll be fine, if I get that hose," Emily's voice was soft, but threatening.

Without any further hesitation, one of the men handed her a small hose with a gentle-spray nozzle and Emily began to wet down Mr. Harper's still form as she waited tensely for the Code Blue team. She knew this was more than the small burn center at Ridge could handle. Mr. Harper would probably be stabilized and then transferred to one of the city's huge burn centers. If he lived, Mr. Harper was going to require months of in-hospital care, and then years of therapy. He was going to suffer more for that last cigarette than even the devil himself would have thought possible.

Now Emily heard the municipal fire department's team racing through the halls, the distinctive clink of their gear preceding them through the hallway, but not by much—they were at a dead run.

"Do we evacuate the rest of the patients from this floor?" Denise asked the captain, stepping aside so that the firemen could enter the room.

The captain nodded. "At least this wing. Get 'em out of here for the time being. It's safest that way."

The firemen moved efficiently through the room, tearing down what was left of the wall, making certain there were no pockets of heat smoldering that could flare up later.

"Out of the way, please!"

The Code Blue team had arrived. Their special carts held all the equipment necessary to keep a critical patient alive and safe until he or she had been transferred. The code team handled everything from heart attacks and strokes to burns. At least this patient hadn't been sprayed all over with burn

10

ointment—dealing with burns was most effective when the surface of the skin was clean.

"Saline soaks," the doctor muttered as he went to work, packing Mr. Harper's body with clean moist soaks that would hopefully minimize the damage. "Thank you for keeping him wet, nurse," he added quietly. "Establish an IV line, start lactated ringers." The work flowed smoothly around what was left of the hospital bed.

"I'm going to have to do a femoral cutdown—I can't get an IV started. Or we could go cutdown and central line," the resident from emergency announced. Ridge's team always had a specialist who could find a vein where none apparently existed; usually they were residents who were brash, confident, and extremely good at their work. The resident winced as he felt for something, *anything*, that would give him an indication of the location of a viable vein. As far as he could tell, Mr. Harper's veins had simply disappeared. There wasn't even a hint of a place where he could start the solution that was desperately needed to keep Mr. Harper alive. He was aware that shock from loss of fluids was more likely to kill the man than almost anything else. If fluid resuscitation didn't start soon, they'd lose Mr. Harper.

"This guy is in severe burn shock—his veins have collapsed so thoroughly there isn't a sign of them anywhere," the resident said, shaking his head.

"Establishing airways," the respiratory therapist announced.

"He's shocky, down to—damn it, I've lost it!" the resident said in frustration. The blood pressure had, as far as he could tell, just dropped to zero. Then, "No, we've got a surge—it's back!"

There was a short, tense silence.

"Come *on*!" the therapist said, as she tried again.

"It's gone again. We're losing him . . . systolic down to forty-five, pulse is one twenty-five."

"I can't intubate him. We're going to have to trach him," Claire, the respiratory therapist said. Since she wasn't going to be able to pass a thin tube carrying lifesaving oxygen down the man's burned throat, his only hope was literally to have his throat cut, opening an airway in the center of his neck where a tube could be established and oxygen could start to keep the lungs going. Claire had seen burns like this before. There was only a tiny airway still open; the rest of the lining of the throat and mouth had been burned away in the flash of the original oxygen fire.

"Do it!" the physician ordered. He knew that Claire was as competent as any doctor. She had done more trachs in emergency than most doctors ever had a chance to see. If anyone could get an airway established, she would be the one. The doctor looked over at the monitor and gritted his teeth.

"No pulse!"

The respiratory therapist paused, her hand poised above Mr. Harper's neck. One finger marked the spot where part of the airway was nearest the skin.

"Laryngoscope and trach tube ready," one of the other nurses said quietly.

Claire hesitated, her scalpel resting against Harper's burned skin.

"He's gone," the doctor said wearily. There was no point in trying heroic measures that might have brought him back—Mr. Harper had simply lost too much fluid. Emily had done everything right, including hosing the man down, but it had probably been too late the instant the fire had blown and incinerated him.

Slowly the team began to disconnect the various

systems they had been ready to attach to Mr. Harper. There was no buzz of conversation.

"Chief?" Denise hurried back into the room. She had been out tending to the other patients and trying to keep several of them from going into hysterics.

The fireman turned toward the head nurse, obviously glad for the interruption. He didn't like death in any form, and he liked it even less when it resulted from a fire. He'd had his share of taking bodies out of buildings in bags, but he had never become inured to seeing what some of the men called "crispy critters." It was a painful kind of humor, a funny name for a terrible tragedy.

"I've started moving the other patients to different sections of the hospital," Denise told him. "We've put the patients who aren't ambulatory in a different wing. If necessary, we could get them downstairs, but it looked like the fire was under control."

"That's fine. We're going to be here for a while, mopping up and making certain there aren't any hot spots, but these buildings are meant to be fire resistant. Even if something does get started, it wouldn't burn for long—at least that's the theory," the captain said.

"I'll take care of the patients. Let me know if you need anything," Denise said briskly.

Emily stood aside, looking at Mr. Harper one last time. She knew it was uncharitable and she wouldn't have told anyone in the world what she was thinking, but she couldn't feel sorry for the man. He had been stupid, and his death had been stupid. At least, she thought, he hadn't suffered those last few minutes. Burn victims don't start to feel the pain until later. Mr. Harper had never had a later. . . .

"Denise, Mrs. Mallow is threatening to leave the

hospital right now, and never mind that she's supposed to go in for tests tomorrow. Says she'd rather live with a bleeding ulcer than this." Nancy indicated the devastated room with a wave of her hand.

"Check whether there's room on three, would you? It's nice, it's quiet, and she'll relax—I hope. And tell Keith to please make certain that all the patients' records are okay. I'm having nightmares, thinking about the papers that got ruined. I hope everyone has a good memory," Denise said grimly.

"I'll tell Keith," Nancy said. She glanced over at Emily, who would have to stay with the patient until an orderly arrived and moved the body to the morgue.

This time, the orderly from downstairs was quick and efficient. Emily figured that he probably wanted to see what had happened on six. In a matter of thirty minutes, it was all over. The only trace that Mr. Harper had been in the room were a few blackened pages of his mystery novel.

Emily walked back toward the nurses' station, her heavy white shoes squeaking and squishing from the water that had poured down over everything. She was thoroughly drenched, but she didn't care. She felt as though she were walking on eggs, trying to keep from screaming and running out of the hospital and never coming back. No one knew what an effort it had been to stay there in that room with fire all around her. She trembled violently with the memories that the sound, the smell, the feel of the fire had reawakened. She had finally encountered the worst that could happen to her in a hospital and in her life, and it had almost undone her.

"You all right, sweetie?" Keith looked over at her as he picked up the wet pages of the reports that the nurses had been writing when the disaster hit. He was hanging them on a board to dry, if possible, before placing them in the charts.

"I'm all right," Emily quavered.

"Sure you are. Everyone goes around with dead white skin, and eyes the size of saucers."

"It just brought back—memories, that's all," Emily said and started to pick up more papers.

Suddenly her hand started to shake uncontrollably, and then her arms, and then her whole body.

"Hey . . ." Keith swooped down and grabbed her just as she fell to the floor.

"Now don't you tell me *that's* all right. Woman, you're in bad shape!"

Emily closed her eyes, resting against Keith.

"It was the fire. My first husband died in a fire. . . . I was with him. The car burned, and it was the same sound—that sudden *whoosh* and then the heat . . ." Emily started to cry.

Keith looked up and caught Denise's eye as the head nurse came over to them.

"Get her downstairs to one of the other lounges, have somebody take care of her burns, and then come back," Denise snapped. She was sorry that Emily was having trouble, but she didn't have time to be sympathetic right at the moment. There were still patients to be moved, firemen to deal with, a thousand and one things that had to be attended to. She'd worry about Emily later, if she had time.

Emily pushed Keith's arms away. She'd prove to Denise that she could stand on her own and could take care of patients. Right now, what she needed was to be around other people, not cooped up in a lounge where all she would think about was death and fire. Left alone, she was certain she'd have a good case of hysterics, and that would help no one.

"Denise, just tell me what you need done, and I'll

do it. Then, when it's all over, I'm going to go home and have a good long cry and several stiff drinks!" Emily said.

Denise smiled briefly. That was why she liked Emily—she could always count on her, no matter what the crisis. That was what made a good nurse even better.

Chapter Two

Emily was still shaking when she opened the door to her home. She had never in all her years as a nurse lived through such a crazy night. The memory of Mr. Harper lying on the bed, his skin crisped and blackened, and the jet of flame rushing toward her was almost more than she could bear.

She was glad to retreat to the peace and quiet of her own house and her own family. She could hear water rushing in the bathroom as her six-year-old daughter Colleen bathed and readied herself for school. In the kitchen, Emily's housemate and helper, Nora Dominic, sang a popular country-western love song as she prepared breakfast. Wonderful smells of warm bread and frying bacon filled the hallway. It was a perfectly normal, perfectly wonderful morning, Emily told herself. There wasn't any sickness, there wasn't any death, there weren't too many problems. There also wasn't a husband, but she didn't miss her former second husband, Nicholas, a bit.

Nora was responsible for putting together the morning meal, and she did it with great gusto, and more than a touch of the down-home country cooking she had been used to on the farm in Kansas. As far as the diminutive legal secretary was concerned, no breakfast was complete without potatoes, some kind of meat or chicken, toast and marmalade, and thick cream in the coffee. Emily had chided her often enough about cholesterol and heart disease, but Nora always countered with a cholesterol count far under the normal average, so Emily had given up. She had finally decided that there was no fighting with success. Besides, coming home to something cooking was comforting, and Emily had needed comfort more than she cared to admit in these last six months since her divorce from Nicholas. She sagged against the wall for a moment, taking time to savor the sense of security that surrounded her.

"That you, Emily?" Nora asked. Her voice was flat and brisk and identified her immediately as being from the Midwest. Nora's back was turned to the nurse as Emily walked into the kitchen. She flipped over the strips of bacon that were frying and said over her shoulder, "Things were quiet last night. Colleen was a good girl—went right to bed on time, which makes me wonder if something's wrong with her." She expertly flipped over an egg.

It was a standing joke between the two women that nothing short of a cataclysmic illness would ever make Colleen go to bed on time. The little girl was a whirlwind—at six years old, she had more energy than Nora and her mother put together.

Nora reached for the plates, standing on tiptoes because she was so short that anything above counter

18

level was almost out of reach for her. She had already cooked french toast, and the heavenly smell of real home-brewed, freshly ground coffee filled the kitchen.

"That smells so good that I could eat at least ten pieces of toast. And a gallon of coffee wouldn't be bad, either," Emily said. Her voice was as tired as the rest of her, and the feeling of interest and excitement that she usually radiated was missing this morning.

Nora turned from the stove, carrying a plate of french toast and bacon for Emily. She took one look at her friend and let out a little screech, almost dropping the plate of food on the floor.

"Good Lord a'mighty, woman, what happened to you?" She stared at Emily's frizzed and slightly burned dark hair that usually lay like a neat, curly cap around her head. The bruise on her cheek was an angry purple. Her uniform was singed from the fire, and what wasn't singed was blackened with soot and still wet. "Emily Greer, what happened to you? Where did you get that bruise? And you hardly have any eyebrows left!"

"There was a fire," Emily said wearily. She sank into a chair, leaned forward, and folded her arms on the table, resting her head on them. She knew she smelled of fire and burned flesh, but she was so tired she didn't think she could stand up and walk to the bathroom to take a shower.

"My word! Here, you just drink this coffee and eat a bite or two and you'll feel better. I'll take Colleen to school this morning on my way to work," Nora said, ordering Emily around as if she were as much her charge as Colleen.

"Thanks," Emily sighed. How very like Nora, she thought, not to question her about the night or the fire. Nora knew that Emily would talk when the time was right. Until then, there would be no pressure, no hounding her for details, nothing but a friendly cup of coffee and an offer of help. Nora's calm acceptance of almost everything was what made her an ideal housemate and friend. Trying to pool resources and time with anyone else would have been unthinkable.

Emily ate a few bites of french toast, liberally doused with maple syrup. The freshly ground coffee lived up to its hot, bitter promise. Within ten minutes Emily had revived enough to think about cleaning herself up. It was the lingering smell of the fire that finally drove her to the bathroom which Colleen had vacated, and the warm water in the shower.

She stripped off her uniform, put what was left of it in a plastic bag, and stood in front of the mirror, examining herself. All night she had been itching, and now she could see why—there were flakes of burned material all over her skin.

"I didn't burn," she said aloud in surprise. Emily held out her arms and looked at them. She had expected to see patches of dead white, or at least blisters from the flames, but she was miraculously unscathed except for the cut that had been treated at the hospital, and the bruise on her face. Otherwise, she was just plain dirty, and she smelled.

That smell—God, she remembered it so well from the wreck that had taken Brad's life. The sound of metal ripping into metal, a screech and then a thud, and the sudden flames crackling into life around her. The smell of burning flesh . . .

There had been no warning as the other car ran the red light and smashed into the small foreign car that Brad had insisted upon buying because it was cheap and efficient. The side caved in, the metal shredding under the impact of the older, heavier vehicle. There had been a moment when they skidded out of control, the car pinwheeling, sparks flying and metal screaming, and then there was the soft *whoomp* as fire engulfed the vehicle.

Emily could remember shouting to her husband to get out as she struggled to loosen the seat belt that had kept her in the car during the accident and the spin-out, but there had been no response. Thinking that Brad had only been knocked unconscious, Emily tried to free him from the seat belt and pull him from the car herself. She knew he was hurt and that she had to save him. Desperately Emily reached over, putting her hand directly into the fire to try and release him. The safety harness popped free and Brad slumped sideways against her. It was only then that she saw that half his face was gone. The same impact that had torn the car to shreds had flayed the skin from the underlying bone and muscle.

She remembered screaming, the sound tearing out of her throat. They had plans; they had to get to the store and then take the car for new tires, and they were going to pick up a kitten from one of their friends. It *couldn't* be over! Not her Brad, not the only man she had ever loved!

But it was over.

"Get out! Get out!" She could still hear the voices of the people around her. They had come rushing out of the fruit and vegetable store on the corner where the accident had happened. One man was spraying a fire extinguisher over the wreck and another reached into the burning vehicle, frantic to save at least one person from the inferno. Someone grabbed her, pulling her away from Brad. As they staggered back, the car erupted as the gasoline tank finally exploded.

It had taken years to recover from that terrible day, to pick up the threads of her life and go on. The drunk driver who had caused the accident had walked away, only slightly injured. He had served three months in jail, and he had paid nothing at all for the damage he caused, because he had no insurance and no assets that Emily's attorneys could discover.

Emily had not been quite so lucky. Her left hand had been burned so badly that the doctors despaired of ever being able to restore full mobility. They worked with her, though, trying everything possible, because she was one of their own. Gradually she regained the use of her hand. And gradually she came back from the hell she had buried herself in, a hell built of pain and memories. For almost a year, she thought every single day about killing herself. She had dark fantasies about taking a gun and killing drunks like the one who had killed Brad. She read the papers avidly, looking for stories about other people who were going through the same horrors that she had survived. During the long nights, she sat up and quilted. By the time she finished the year, she had finished eight quilts. Her last quilt had been pieced and sewn in blue and white, Brad's favorite colors. She had never been able to look at it again after she clipped the last stitch. It had been her last link with him, and when she finished it, she knew it was time to move on.

Now Emily scrubbed at her hair, washing away the last trace of the fire. She steamed her body, washing again and again until nothing of the scent of death remained.

She had consigned the uniform she'd been wearing to the trash, though she winced at the thought of what she'd paid for it. But there was no help for it—there were holes in the front of the tunic, and the pants had been so badly singed that she was surprised to find that her legs, underneath the fabric, were pink and healthy rather than burned.

"Mommy, I'm going to school! Come and kiss me," Colleen's imperious voice cut through the sound of the shower.

"Mommy, I can't see you, there's so much fog. Come out and kiss me good-bye, or I won't go with Nora!"

Emily smiled and turned off the water. It was all right—she had survived. She would kiss Colleen good-bye, and then she'd fall into bed and sleep for hours. The troubles of the night would finally fade away.

Emily stepped out of the shower and wrapped herself in a towel, savoring the warmth of the room and the scent of the rose lilac soap she had used.

Colleen looked adorable, as usual. Her hair was the same dark shade as her mother's, and she usually wore it in braids. Colleen also had huge brown eyes inherited from her father, Emily's second husband. She had a pixie smile, and radiated energy. Emily often wondered if her daughter would ever go a whole week without a skinned knee or a bruised shin. Colleen was always ready to answer a challenge, and she had seen the inside of the emergency room more than once to be stitched up and given a shot or two.

At least, Emily thought, as she smoothed her daughter's hair, she hasn't broken anything—yet.

"You be a good girl and don't get into any trouble, okay? No more swinging your lunch box at Teddy Rice," Emily warned. She had already received a call at work from the principal about yesterday's fight.

Colleen looked up, her eyes narrowing. "I will if he pulls my braids one more time! I'll knock his block off!"

"Colleen, leave Teddy alone or the principal will yell at me again, and I don't like her telling me I'm raising a half-pint hoodlum," Emily warned.

Colleen stuck out her lower lip. "I am *not* a half-pint!"

"Teddy, watch out," Emily said under her breath.

She kissed her daughter's forehead. It felt slightly warm. Emily frowned. Could there be a tiny fever? And were Colleen's eyes just a bit too bright?

"Do you feel all right, honey?" she asked, concerned that she might be overlooking something.

"I'm fine, Mommy." Colleen squirmed against her mother's embrace, anxious to leave. "I have to go. Sandra and I are going to play marbles this morning before the bell rings," she said impatiently, and darted down the hall and out the back door before Emily could call her back and check her out more thoroughly.

Emily heard the car door slam, then Nora backed the car out of the driveway as she hurried off to Colleen's school and her job.

"It's nothing. There's no fever. Colleen would have said something if she wasn't feeling well," Emily tried to reassure herself. She realized that she was probably overreacting to the night's trauma. For a while, she could expect everything to look more dangerous than it really was. Without thinking, she rubbed at the places on her left hand where the scar tissue had never quite become pliable, even after years of work and rehabilitation.

She wandered into the bedroom, almost missing the note that had been taped to the door.

"Pay the gas and electric and the water bills today."

Nora's stylized handwriting, almost Spenserian in its delicacy, belied the uncompromising message.

"Oh, damn!" Emily groaned. She wasn't prepared to deal with the bills. She knew her bank balance was almost down to zero, and she also knew perfectly well that the bills had to be paid.

Emily glanced up at the clock on her bureau. It was almost eight-thirty. Nicholas, workaholic that he was, should be in his office now. Sometimes, if she was lucky, he'd answer the phone himself because the receptionist and his secretary didn't arrive until nine.

Emily dialed the number and waited, holding her breath.

"Nicholas Greer. May I help you?" the hearty male voice, rich in upper-class Boston accents, came over the wire.

Emily smiled thinly. So she'd guessed right.

"Nicholas, this is Emily," she said.

Nicholas sighed. "Yes, Emily, what do you want this time?" He sounded weary, as if he couldn't stand the thought of having to talk to her. He preferred to deal with her through their lawyers, letting them handle all the sordid details that accompanied their nasty little divorce. He had been delighted with the way his attorney and law partner, Leopold Peters, had handled Emily's wimp of a lawyer. For that reason, Nicholas much preferred to have Leopold do the talking.

"I want the child support that was supposed to have started months ago, and I'd like to have the money due me from the retirement fund. You know, Nicholas, that was supposed to be in my hand the day we signed the papers, and you asked for a little time to settle the other financial odds and ends. I'm through waiting. If you want me to get ugly, I'll go back to my attorney. But I think it would be a lot easier if you just sent the money. And by the way, it would be nice if you'll call Colleen once in a while."

Emily was proud of herself. She'd stated her case in a calm, reasonable manner. She hadn't threatened him, except with more legal action, and she had kept her cool. That in itself was a major accomplishment.

Just the sound of his voice made her want to kick and scream. He had managed to wrest almost everything away from her during the divorce except the house and Colleen. She'd never known what had hit her.

"You'll get your money eventually. Don't panic about it. Leopold won't overlook the agreement we worked out. It'll be there within the next month or so. And, Emily, please don't call me here at the office or at home. If you want to communicate with me, do so through Leopold."

The line went dead in her hand.

"Damn, damn, *damn!*" Emily swore. He'd done it again! He didn't care about her, or about Colleen. He hadn't even asked about his daughter. She should call Frank Dorman, her lawyer, but she was simply too tired, both physically and emotionally, to wrestle with one more problem. Besides, Frank wouldn't be able to force Nicholas to act like a good father.

She went into the living room, sat down at her desk, and pulled out her check book. Her account was so low that she didn't carry checks with her any more. What good would it do to write a check that she knew would only bounce?

The balance stared up at her, the neat writing clear and uncompromising. She had forty-two dollars and eighteen cents left until Friday, and this was only Tuesday.

She took the bills out of the bill box and added them up, knowing ahead of time that she was going to be depressed by the total. She owed over a thousand dollars in essential bills right now, and there was a house payment coming up in the next two weeks. Even with Nora's monthly contribution of six hundred dollars to house expenses, she wasn't going to have anything left over for food if she paid the bills. If she didn't pay the gas and the water and all the other essential services, they were going to be lighting the house with candles, and trying to cadge showers from the neighbors.

There was only one thing to do—call the various companies and ask for mercy. Quickly she dialed the customer service numbers of her outstanding creditors and pleaded for just a little more time. In two weeks, she assured them, she'd be caught up. She crossed her fingers as she talked, knowing that while she might be able to catch up on this month's bills, it was always a dead run between each paycheck and the incoming dunning notices. She'd never be able to pay everything until she collected from Nicholas, and at the moment, that seemed like a very remote possibility.

"What the hell did I ever see in that man?" Emily wondered aloud as she put the bills away.

But she knew full well what it was she had seen in Nicholas. He was handsome, six feet of suntan and smile and dark brown hair. He was forceful, a trait gained from years of arguing in front of a judge. He had sworn that he loved her.

Nicholas had come into her life as a result of the accident that had killed Brad. Someone at the hospital had recommended Peters and Greer as being the best law firm in town for personal injury and wrongful death suits. She had taken down the name, and made an appointment with Nicholas Greer. He was certain there was a way to recover damages from the drunk driver who had caused the accident. After the investigation, which showed that the man who killed Brad had no assets and nothing to lose, Nicholas had stayed in her life. It had started over coffee and progressed to taking her to bed. He had been kind and gentle, and she had been grateful for the human touch. Nicholas had swept her off her feet with his protestations of love and everlasting devotion.

Now, seven years later, Emily could see that the marriage had come too soon—she had not finished grieving for Brad. Suddenly her life had been turned upside down again when she married Nicholas—and almost immediately became pregnant.

Trouble began to brew within the first year. Nicholas wasn't ready to have a child so soon. He'd been married before and his older children were almost ready for college. He didn't relish the idea of another squalling brat around. He had tried to persuade Emily to have an abortion, but had finally dropped the subject when she began to have screaming nightmares about killing her unborn child.

Then there was the issue of her going back to work while she was still undergoing therapy and other surgeries for the burn damage. Nicholas had wanted an ornament in his life, not a working wife. Emily could have the baby, but she couldn't have her job. He'd put up with her stupidity in getting pregnant so soon after the wedding, but he wasn't about to have his wife leave that same infant with a nurse-housekeeper and go back to nursing. There was no room for compromise. He neither cared nor listened when Emily tried to tell him how important her career was to her.

The feuds and troubles had lasted for five years. Looking back on it now, Emily felt that the divorce seemed preordained almost from the moment the minister had pronounced them man and wife.

The phone rang, breaking Emily out of her depressing thoughts.

"Emily, this is Monica Harper, head nurse for days?" the woman's voice had a slight questioning inflection, as if she weren't certain Emily would remember her.

"Hi, Monica, how are you?"

"I'm fine, but I'm also really short-handed today. This flu epidemic has cut into the staff, and I'm two people short."

Emily knew what was coming. Monica wanted her to come back to the hospital and work another shift, back to back with her night shift. It would mean double-time pay, but it would also mean that she would only have three or four hours' sleep, if she were lucky.

"Emily, I hate to ask, but could you come on in? I really need the help."

"What about the agency? Don't they have anyone available?" Emily asked wearily.

"They've already sent all the nurses they can. And besides, you know that we like to give the chance to our own staff first. Not only do you know the hospital, you also know the patients and they'll get better care. Fair enough?"

Emily tried to think of a way she could reasonably decline the offer of the extra time—and the extra money. She was so tired that every bone in her body ached. She was still shaking from the fear that the fire had reawakened. She wanted to sit in her own home with her own things around her and just rest and recuperate from the worst night in her whole nursing career.

On the other hand, she knew that Monica wouldn't have called if the need weren't critical. Certainly Denise Frazier would have told her that Emily had been in the room when the fire had erupted. Monica would have left her alone to recuperate if there had been any other nurse available for the extra assignment.

Emily looked over at the bill box and winced. The bills stuck out of the top of the box like a reproach for her lack of funds. Given just eight hours at double time, she would almost be able to pay the gas and electric bills. And, truthfully, time in the hospital would keep her from thinking about all the problems that were eating away at her.

"I'll be in. Give me a few minutes to get into a clean uniform, and about fifteen minutes to drive back down to the hospital, and you'll have at least one less nurse to worry about," Emily said.

"Oh, thank you, Emily! I can't tell you how much I appreciate your help," Monica said. The relief was evident in her voice. "I'll be looking for you."

Emily took only enough time to call Nora and tell her what was happening. It was a house rule—each of the women left complete information with each other on where they were and what time they would be back. When they had first begun this experiment in living together, the arrangement had smacked of being back in college, in a dormitory that required time checks and signing in and out. Now they both appreciated the security of knowing that someone else always knew where they were and when they expected to be back. In modern city life, checking in with each other was a small price to pay for the safety factor.

"I'll leave something defrosting for dinner, and I'll call the school and have them tell Colleen to go over to Sarah's house until I can pick her up. Everything will work out just fine," Emily said.

"Sounds like it's all under control. Don't wear yourself out," Nora said, her voice brisk and efficient. Emily could hear the sound of the computer keyboard ticking as they talked. Nora always did at least two things at the same time whenever possible. She never talked on the phone without continuing her work at the computer, and she swore she never made a mistake.

Two more calls, and Emily was ready to leave. She locked the door, glad to leave behind the troubles she knew would have overwhelmed her if she had stayed home.

Chapter Three

It took two days before Ridge Six East could be used again for patients. During that time, the halls were cleaned and repainted where the smoke had smudged the walls. Mr. Harper's room had been sealed off and would be rebuilt during the next few weeks by building-maintenance and construction crews. The windows of all the other rooms had been shined, the beds changed, the nurses' station tidied up, and the patients had been brought back into the section that had almost gone up in flames.

It gave Emily an eerie feeling on the third day to look down the hallway and see not one trace of the fire.

"Mrs. Greer, will you pay attention? I know you've been working overtime, but I expect that your level of competence will not be affected while you are caring for my patients. No complaints may have been lodged, but I am warning you right now to listen when I am talking."

Emily gritted her teeth. Dr. Milton O'Shea was pulling his usual prima-donna act. Just looking at him, you knew that here was an Important Man. Over six feet tall, his prematurely white hair, craggy face, and imperious manner let every nurse who had ever encountered him know that he was their absolute superior. He was also a royal pain.

Emily was one of the few nurses at Ridge who regularly stood up to him, and as a result there had been unremitting tension between the two of them for almost six years. Sometimes he could bring himself to be civil to her, but most of the time the thought of being polite never occurred to him.

Now Emily took a deep breath and fixed him with a steely glare. "Dr. O'Shea, your comments are completely unnecessary. Your patients have always been well cared for. Even during the fire, I risked my life going into the room to try and take that cigarette away from *your* patient. You certainly cannot hold me responsible for Mr. Harper's decision to smoke, nor his subsequent death."

"Mrs. Greer, I believe that you were indeed responsible for Mr. Harper's death," O'Shea snapped. "You should have been more alert to the fact that he had access to cigarettes. You should not have permitted him to smoke."

"No nurse can be expected to stand over a patient night and day to keep him from indulging in destructive behavior. We are health-care professionals, not jailers!"

"You knew he was a risk—you just didn't watch him closely enough."

"And *you* didn't search him or his room to make

certain that he didn't have cigarettes," Emily shot back.

"That's not my job," O'Shea said blandly.

"It's not mine, either. If you wanted that kind of constant supervision, then you should have requested someone from security or ordered a private nurse for the man."

Emily had already filled out all the paper work that had been generated by the accident. She knew she was right and Dr. O'Shea was wrong. No matter how much he blustered, the fault lay with Mr. Harper and no one else.

In fact, a great deal of her free time in the past three days had been spent filling out the required hospital reports on how and why the accident had happened. There were reports on what had happened physically to cause the fire and what had happened while the fire was burning. Emily had been asked to write down her reason for not having been in the room when Mr. Harper lit his fatal cigarette. She knew that within the next few days after the incident reports had been reviewed, she would have to speak directly with the director of nursing administration to explain yet again the sequence of events that night. Administration had the right to question her; O'Shea did not.

"I suppose that I'm going to have to follow you around, making certain that you watch the patients, and change their IVs and follow doctor's orders, right? Isn't that what you're telling me? You can't be held responsible for patients' care? You can't be trusted with difficult cases like Mr. Harper?"

Emily didn't have time for this idiocy. Talking to Dr. O'Shea was like talking to a wall, and about as productive. "Dr. O'Shea, if you have questions about my actions before and during the fire, I suggest you take it up with administration. If you have questions regarding my competence or my record on patient care, I suggest that same action be taken. But you will *not* stand here and insult me as if I were responsible for the fact Mr. Harper had a death wish!" She glared at him, her eyes blazing. "As a matter of fact, I think a good case could be made for negligence on your part for not having warned the administration and the nursing staff that Mr. Harper had a history of attempting to smoke while he was hospitalized."

"It is not my concern."

"Fine, then it isn't mine, either. If you will excuse me, I have no more time to discuss this with you," Emily said firmly.

O'Shea, mortally offended, turned and stalked down the hallway, his leonine head held high.

Emily knew he'd be furious with her for months and his rage would be reflected in his reports on her, but at least she had managed to break off his tirade today.

"Thank God for small mercies," Emily murmured.

She nodded to Keith Jennings as they passed in the hall. If he'd overheard the exchange, he didn't say anything. From the sheets in Keith's hand, she guessed that one of the patients hadn't quite made it to the bathroom. Accidents of that type happened more frequently than most people would suspect in a hospital. Patients weren't used to being encumbered with IV poles and the machines which monitored and dispensed metered doses of medication into the IV lines. Bodies that normally would have responded to the owner's commands simply couldn't move very fast. Aches and pains slowed up even the most vigorous patients. Sometimes the accident was caused by simple physics. Patients didn't understand that for every drop that went into the veins with an IV, fluid in the system would eventually have to be excreted. As a result, nurses spent a fair amount of time changing beds during the night.

As she walked past the open door to room 632, she heard Keith talking to patient Coralie Cooper.

"Now, don't you worry, honey. It was nothing at all. And look at you, awake and beautiful even at this time of night!" Keith said as he walked into the room with the new sheets for her bed. The old woman had been moved to a chair, but even so she was clearly uncomfortable in her wet nightgown.

In truth, she didn't look good at all, Keith thought. Her wrinkles seemed more pronounced tonight and the usually animated blue eyes were hazy with pain. Her hands, bent into claws, lay outside the blanket that Keith had wrapped around her. Coralie had been in for almost a week, and she was deteriorating instead of getting better. She had come in with the flu and it had progressed to an agonizing bout of arthritis.

Coralie shook her head. "Thanks for the compliment, though I know better," she said weakly. She could see for herself that she didn't look good at all. Even her nice new pink nightgown didn't bring out the roses in her cheeks.

"I don't tell women they're looking good if they look like warmed-over tuna fish, but I'm telling you, you are looking *great*. Now, let me get your pulse and respiration here, and then I'll check the IV line. If everything is all right, I think we'd better change you into another gown and make the bed, okay?"

"Cut the 'we,' Keith. *You're* going to be doing all the work," Coralie said tartly. She liked Keith, but she hated hospitals and the nurses who constantly used the plural when they meant the singular patient.

She wasn't going to be a "we" until she saw the nurses taking an enema right alongside her!

"I don't think I'm going to sleep at all tonight," Coralie added. "First I do something foolish like wet the bed, when I haven't done that for eighty years, and then I hurt in every bone in my body. It's this doggoned arthritis attack. I'm twisted into a U shape and my fingers won't bend, and I can't do a damned thing about it. Here it is, spring, and there are a hundred seed catalogues sitting at home on the entryway table, and I can't move my hands good enough to write out an order, much less plant the damn seeds once they come in. I'm a fine mess, young man, and don't you try and tell me otherwise!"

"I know, it's too bad. But everything will get better soon. The one thing about arthritis is that the pain can usually be controlled, and Dr. Mendelsohn has no intention of seeing you in pain," Keith said cheerfully as he made the bed with brisk efficiency. "Are you feeling up to a change of gowns now? I remember seeing a nice fluffy lavender one in your closet. How about putting that on before you get chilled? If you like, I could call Emily in and have her help you while I finish up here."

Keith was careful always to give female patients, particularly older female patients, the chance to have a female staff member take care of any personal hygiene that needed to be attended to. He had learned when he first became a nurse that some women were simply too modest and too quiet to state their objection to a male nurse handling their needs. They would accept being made uncomfortable rather than speaking out, so he always gave the women a choice.

"Actually, Keith, if you'd be kind enough to help me into the shower, I'd like to have a nice long, hot rinse. That water does help the pain of the arthritis sometimes, and Dr. Mendelsohn said he approved of my getting up and walking around as much as possible."

"A shower it is. Let me get it ready, and then you can sit and let the water run over you until you're nice and warm and comfortable."

Keith was pleased that the woman hadn't asked for Emily. He wouldn't have been upset by the request, but he hated to have to turn to Emily or Denise Frazier for help. It could have been interpreted as a failing on his part—female nurses did not usually request male nurses for male patients.

"Once you're out of there and your cheeks are pink again, we'll look into getting you something for the pain and to help you sleep. It's against my code of honor as a nurse to let a sweet lady like you miss a good night's sleep."

Coralie couldn't help smiling.

Keith worked efficiently, taking the shower mat, three large towels, and a washcloth from the closet. When he had collected a fresh bar of soap and Mrs. Cooper's bath slippers that she insisted upon wearing, they were ready for the trek across the hall. He went over to the bathroom, and turned on the faucets full force. Knowing the hospital water pipes, he estimated it would take a good five minutes before the water was warm enough for a comfortable shower.

Keith picked up the elderly woman's wrist and began to count pulse and respiration. After a quick check of her chest to assure that everything was clear, he was ready to escort her into the shower.

Keith wrote the vital signs down on the sheet of paper. Physically, he thought, she was beginning to look better, although it was clear that the move from the bed to the chair had given her pain. Everything was within normal range, so he helped her into the shower and settled her underneath the warm spray. The IV monitor and bag had been wheeled in beside the shower and the arm with the IV had been wrapped in plastic so the water wouldn't loosen the tape or cause other problems.

Keith took the chance to check on several other patients, always coming back to Mrs. Cooper every few seconds and talking to her through the door to make certain she wasn't having any trouble.

Through it all, Keith felt a kind of warm satisfaction in the job that he was doing. He didn't mind the wet beds, the constant running, the complications that his patients presented him with. All his life he had wanted to be a nurse. It was sheer luck that by the time he could go to school, male nurses had become less of an oddity and more of an accepted fact in most hospitals. He knew that some people spent most of their lives trying to find out what job they would be happy doing, and Keith felt immensely lucky that he had found his true calling so early in life.

Within ten minutes he had Mrs. Cooper back in bed, settled and ready for her pill. She looked much more comfortable now than she had when she rang the bell for help.

"Now, Coralie, you stay right there and I'll be back with something to help you sleep, all right?" He patted her gently on the arm and left the room.

"Keith Jennings!" the voice was so close and so virulent that it made him jump as if he'd been stung by an electrical prod. Keith pivoted and stared at the plain young woman who had been standing outside the room, obviously listening. Dr. Shelby glared at him, her pale blue eyes glittering behind her glasses.

She held a chart close to her chest, hunching her thin body slightly over the battered wood.

"Mr. Jennings, what the *hell* do you think you were doing with that patient in there?"

Keith stepped back involuntarily, surprised at the menace in the resident's manner.

"With Mrs. Cooper? I was helping her back into bed after her shower," Keith said warily. He didn't like Dr. Rachel Shelby. She lived up to everything he had always heard about female doctors. She was known for backbiting, and had no bedside manner to speak of. Worst of all, she was obnoxious to everyone on the floor except her immediate superior, Dr. O'Shea. Keith had been on the wrong end of her cutting tongue a few times, and had no wish to repeat the experience.

"You know perfectly well what I mean. Are you not aware, sir, that there are rules of conduct for a nurse?"

"Of course I am aware of professional conduct. I believe I have adhered to the rules," Keith said carefully, trying desperately to remember what he had been saying to Coralie Cooper that could have aroused Dr. Shelby's ire.

"Then you should know that flirting with patients is unprofessional! It is a serious enough offense that a complaint could be registered with the nursing administration," Dr. Shelby said stiffly. She leaned even further toward him, her loose man's shirt opening slightly. She was obviously unaware that even with the chart clasped to her bosom, the shirt gaped just enough to show that, like many militant feminists, she didn't wear a bra.

Keith saw the shirt gap open, and his instant, humorous thought was that Dr. Shelby wasn't making a statement by not wearing a bra—she was simply showing that she had nothing to make a statement *with*. Then he focused on what the doctor had just said.

"Flirting with the patient? What are you talking about?"

"Telling Mrs. Cooper that she looks good, patting her on the arm before you leave the room—such unprofessional conduct could even be cause for dismissal. At the very least, that kind of action gives Ridge Hospital a bad name. Male nurses, in particular, must be especially careful to project the right image. And the right image is not telling older women how pretty they are and touching them when it isn't necessary!"

Keith pressed his lips together in an attempt to keep his temper, or from laughing out loud in disbelief. He wanted to respond to Dr. Shelby, but didn't dare. He'd already had enough run-ins with the Shelby-O'Shea team. He and Shelby's advisor, Dr. O'Shea, were old enemies. Dr. O'Shea had been so incensed the first time Keith had come into the operating room that he had made Keith's life miserable, so Keith had given up and transferred to Six East. Dr. Shelby had taken that as a signal that it was open season on Keith. She had done more than her share of sniping in the last few months until it had almost reached the proportions of outright warfare.

Keith recognized the problem, but wasn't certain that he wanted to lodge a formal complaint about discrimination. In the real world, a black male nurse was always going to have trouble. Keeping his voice level, he said, "I am completely professional, Doctor. However, it may have escaped your notice that patients of both sexes and all ages do better when they are reassured that being ill has not made them less attractive to those around them. That is particularly important when dealing with a person who has just had an embarrassing accident."

"Accidents are not the issue here. The issue here is a form of sexist, sexual banter that should not be permitted," Dr. Shelby insisted stubbornly. Her pale blue eyes shifted away, and she brushed back her limp brown hair with one hand. "You must attempt to keep your 'flirting' under control, Mr. Jennings, or I will report you!"

Dr. Shelby turned and stalked away from the nurse, not giving him a chance to respond to her threat.

Keith took a deep breath and let it out slowly. Dr. Shelby was wrong. He knew instinctively which patients needed to be cheered up and shown they were still acceptable in polite society, no matter how sick they had become. And nothing could make a patient who was sensitive go downhill faster than to have a doctor or nurse who responded negatively to the patient's physical appearance.

Just last week, he had been specifically requested by old Mrs. Adamson. She knew she was dying; she knew that cancer had been eating away at her insides, but it had been discovered too late to try anything at all. The surgeons had just sewn her back up and were ready to send her home to die. Mrs. Adamson had requested that Keith take care of her on the night shift because he made her feel good. She had died that night, and he had been sorry to see her go, but happy that he had eased her last few hours. Mrs. Adamson had had no one left in her family, and she would have died alone, feeling ugly and sick and old and unloved, if Keith had not gently reassured her she was still a remarkable, intelligent, attractive person.

"What the hell is going on with Shelby and O'Shea? They're both in miserable moods," Emily said as she came up to the nurses' station where Keith was writing in Coralie Cooper's chart.

"I have no idea. Someone ought to put a muzzle on O'Shea and cut Shelby off at the knees. Imagine, complaining because I told a woman patient she was looking good!"

"Maybe it's because no one in Dr. Shelby's entire life has ever told her that *she* looks good. She's probably jealous of an eighty-year-old woman," Emily said, grinning.

Keith ran his hand over his chin, wondering if that could really be the problem. If it was, he wasn't about to take on the job of making Shelby believe she was good-looking. He could lie, but not that much.

"I can't feel sorry for her. She shouldn't be told she's attractive when she's a witch in training," Keith said, in an uncharacteristic show of anger.

Emily looked at Keith closely. He was beginning to show the strain. She had known Keith for longer than almost anyone else on the floor. She knew he was black and proud of it, but that information had come as a surprise to more than one nurse and patient on Ridge Six East. He was handsome, with dark hair, dark eyes, and light skin which could have been interpreted as deeply tanned or Mediterranean. Keith was extraordinarily tall and well built, obviously strong. His wrestling days might be over since he had graduated from nursing school and no longer needed the extra income from appearing in the ring, but his heavy neck and broad shoulders testified to his excellent physical condition. In other words, Emily thought, he was altogether gorgeous. But tonight he looked very tired.

"You heard Dr. O'Shea when he lit into me earlier for letting Mr. Harper light a cigarette and blow himself to kingdom come? I guess he thinks we have all the time in the world to act as prison guards in addition to our nursing duties. O'Shea is a martinet, and Shelby takes her cues from him."

Keith nodded his head. "I know it's not just me. But doctors like Shelby sure make other offers look good."

"Other offers?"

"For different nursing jobs somewhere else."

Emily wasn't surprised. About once every three months offers from other hospitals and patient-care facilities came in to every nurse on the floor. There was a chronic shortage of qualified staff, and more than one professional had been induced to leave Ridge for greener, better-paying pastures.

"There's a neurological-care facility opening up. I might go in and talk to them. It's more money, and I'd be in charge of a unit. And best of all, there'd be no more Dr. Shelby. That in itself makes the deal worth looking into."

Denise Frazier stopped at the nurses' station for a moment, interrupting their conversation.

"Keith, the chest people up on eight are transferring a patient down from the Constant Care rooms. Seems there's been a rash of accidents, and the beds are needed for new traumas. Anyway, you've got him—patient's name is John Alvarez."

Keith dropped the papers he had been holding, and slapped the top of the counter. "What was the name again?"

"John Alvarez," Denise repeated, wondering what on earth was wrong with Keith.

"He's been up in Constant Care? What happened?

45

Do we have any more info at all?" His face was tense, and his hands were clenched. It couldn't be! There had to be at least a hundred John Alvarezes in the city. Wouldn't someone have told him?

Emily shrugged and then pointed toward the door.

"They're being efficient tonight—here comes the patient right now."

Chapter Four

"God, please let it be somebody else . . . ," Keith muttered as he walked forward to intercept the gurney-pushers from the eighth floor.

"New patient—where do you want him?" The escort handed Keith the patient records in the heavy aluminum cover. Keith looked at the name, then at the face, and flinched.

It was John Alvarez, all right. His dark, curly hair was mussed, and he badly needed a haircut. But it was the same thin, aquiline face that never aged. John had always looked ten years younger than he really was, and he was the one who had invariably been carded when the three best friends wanted to go into a bar. Keith Jennings, Bill Sonderson, and John Alvarez were all the same age. They had gone to school together, studied together, and partied together. They were a team, and now something terrible had happened to one of them.

Keith fought to keep his emotions under control. God, John looked bad! His color was a pasty yellow that looked even worse against the institutional greenish white of the pillow case. The black eyes that usually sparkled with interest and enthusiasm about everything under the sun were closed, and the mouth that always smiled was flaccid. The Ivac pumped fluids into his body as the green light marching across the face of the monitor told everyone John's IV line was working, and he was getting the lifesaving antibiotics that were marked on the white tape on the glucose bag.

"History?" Keith managed to ask the accompanying nurse. Something to do with the chest, that was obvious. Had he collapsed while playing racquetball? Had he been in a car wreck? Why hadn't Bill Sonderson called and let him know that their pal was being admitted to the very hospital where Keith worked?

"Gunshot wound, left lobe. He was doing fine until he showed symptoms of pneumonia. O'Shea did the original surgery to examine and close the wound. One day later, *wham*—there it was, high fever, chest pain, and all these patches on the X ray. It hit him hard. Says in the chart that he developed acute bacterial pneumonia, but he's recovering." The nurse didn't show any emotion as she described the case. To her, he was just another patient to be cared for, without investing any emotion in the caring. John Alvarez meant nothing to her.

"Thanks," Keith said. He didn't trust himself to say anything more. Why hadn't Bill called him? Why hadn't anyone told him that one of the three musketeers was lying two floors above him, dying from a gunshot wound? He would have gone up there and watched the case himself, stayed extra hours, substituted for any nurses who wanted a day off in the Constant Care Unit. That was how close Bill and John and Keith had been.

Then Keith remembered that his answering machine had broken sometime in the last two weeks—if Bill had tried to reach him, the phone would simply have rung without the machine kicking in. He had thought it was kind of nice to come home to no messages that had to be returned. Never again! That machine was going to be repaired the instant he got home.

Keith escorted the team to 640 and helped them move his friend onto the bed. There wasn't a flicker of consciousness from John as they rearranged his body, changed the IV bag, and set up the tube system that kept the fluid draining out of the chest wound until the lung had a chance to heal.

"Keith, the lady at the desk said you were in here . . . I need your help. We've got to find . . ." Bill Sonderson hurried into the room and then skidded to a stop. He looked at the body on the bed and whispered, "You've found him!"

"Bill, what the hell is going on? A gunshot wound? Why didn't you tell me? How long has he been in here?"

"I'll tell you about it later. Right now, make sure that John is among the living, okay? And then, as soon as you have time, we've got to have a small discussion about this hospital," Bill said grimly.

Keith nodded and turned back to John. Bill was right—there would be time enough to talk later. He leaned over to check the chest tube system to make certain it was working. Normally the machine was reliable, but it had been known to malfunction. He checked the water level by pinching off the tube and waiting for the bubbling in the unit to stop. The water level checked out at twenty—enough pressure to keep things working properly. The system was moved to the new bed and placed below chest level. For a moment, Keith looked at his friend and thought once again how frail he looked. It was as if John had never developed beyond that first flush of manhood at twenty-one. He was small and wiry and tough, and still only about half the size of Keith. Keith checked the amount of drainage from the tube.

"When did you say this was last checked?" Keith asked the nurse who had come down with the patient. Surely the notes on the chamber were wrong.

"I didn't. But it was about an hour ago." She rolled her eyes. Couldn't the man read?

"And it's up to a hundred twenty already? Isn't that a little high?" Keith knew perfectly well that any drainage over one hundred milliliters per hour into the chamber was a danger sign. He couldn't understand why the attending nurses hadn't caught it even before John was prepped for the move. He touched John's forehead and drew his hand back in alarm. The man was burning up!

"Can't help it. Call the doc yourself if you want, but Shelby had orders from O'Shea to bring this man down and move another patient into his bed, and that's just what I did. I'm not going to make any fuss about it—the charge nurse already did that and all it got her was a chewing out from that bug-eyed excuse for a doctor." The nurse was washing her hands of the case, handing the problem over to Keith. She didn't want to fuss with the man any longer. He wasn't her patient and it wasn't her floor.

Bill Sonderson stayed quietly in the background, listening. He had switched on the small pocket recorder that he carried at all times, just in case a story developed. As city editor of the Chicago *Mercury*, he was constantly on the lookout for trouble.

"Sign here, please," the nurse from eight said, pushing the papers at Keith.

"Let's hold off on that, okay?" Keith said tightly. He ran the probe from the thermometer into another casing and placed it beneath John's tongue again. Surely that couldn't be right—Shelby wouldn't be stupid enough to send a man down to a general nursing floor with a chest tube and a temperature of 104. The thermometer beeped, and he saw that the temperature had already inched up to 104.2. A quick listen to the chest, with all the extra sounds and the definite rales of pneumonia made him shake his head. John's pulse was rapid, and he was breathing in short, inefficient bursts.

"You've got to sign for the patient," the nurse insisted.

"Just wait, all right? Don't get pushy!" Now that he'd completed his workup, Keith didn't like what he was seeing at all.

"Come on, damn it, don't be hard to get along with," the nurse said testily. She didn't like it when any man threw his weight around, and she wasn't going to stand for it from Keith, nurse or no nurse.

"I said, *in a while,*" Keith said, and looked the nurse straight in the eye. He had no intention of signing anything until Denise had a chance to look at John Alvarez. "I want my supervisor to check the patient over. If you have something else to do, you can go upstairs, work awhile and then come back for the papers, or you can go on coffee break. But I'm not accepting this patient until Denise Frazier has had a chance to evaluate his condition."

"Suit yourself. I'm due for a break now anyway,

and there's nothing to make me hurry right back upstairs," the nurse said, shrugging. She put the paper back under the pillow. She wasn't going to get herself in an uproar just because Keith didn't want to sign the transfer papers. Like it or not, the patient was on his floor, in his bed, and Mr. Macho Nurse was going to have to deal with it.

"Denise, could I have your help in here for a minute?" Keith leaned out the door and asked the charge nurse, who was seated at the desk right across the hall.

"Sure, what have you got?"

"New patient. What did they tell you about him when they phoned from upstairs to see if we had a bed available?"

Denise hurried into the room—she never walked when she could run. She was always in a hurry.

"They told me it was a gunshot wound. I remember reading something about it in the papers yesterday." Denise shook her head, commiserating with the unconscious man in the bed and thinking that it could have been her just as easily as John Alvarez— drug dealers weren't careful about who happened to be standing around when they let loose with their barrage of fire.

"Apparently this man was in the wrong place at the wrong time when some crack dealers decided to shoot it out. He was brought into emergency and right into surgery. Word from upstairs was that he's stable and is ready to be transferred out to a regular floor instead of staying in pulmonary constant care," Denise answered as she went to the patient and began to take his vitals again herself. "Lousy break for this guy, though," she continued as she worked. "I remember thinking that things have definitely gotten out of hand when scum like that start shooting right outside one of the city's best restaurants. He was inside, you know, not out on the street. Naturally, when I heard about it, my first reaction was that of a nurse—I wondered if he'd eaten or if he was brought in with an empty stomach. I was hoping for empty stomach, because of course that makes it so much easier to give him anesthetic for the surgery."

She frowned, and took the vitals again.

"What's going on here? I'm getting his temp as one hundred four. That's way too high. And listen to the heart—it's really racing right along."

She flipped up his eyelid, and shone the light into the pupil.

"Damn, he's got the darkest eyes I've ever seen! It's hard to see where the pupil leaves off and the rest of the eye begins," Denise complained. "Pupils look responsive, but it's a very slow response. How is he to stimulus?"

"Let me give it a try," Keith said. He moved to the side of the bed while Denise took out the chart and noted her findings, then flipped back to the medications page to see if anything John Alvarez was getting would account for the slowed pupil response. She and Keith had long since forgotten that Bill Sonderson was still in the room.

"Hey, buddy! John, wake up, I've got to talk to you!" Keith shook his friend's shoulder, hoping for some sign that John could hear him. There was a faint flicker of the eyelids and the patient groaned, but otherwise he did not respond.

"John, wake up right now!" Denise took over, her voice sharp and penetrating. Keith was being too gentle. She knew from years of experience with patients who were under sedation that a good loud,

raucous voice did wonders to wake them up. Sometimes it was necessary to be almost brutal in getting a
response.

She grabbed his hand and pinched one of the
fingers, not hard enough to draw blood, but definitely enough to rouse a person who was sensitive to
pain stimulus.

John Alvarez groaned again and his eyes slowly
opened, staring uncomprehendingly toward the ceil-
ing.

Keith let out a breath that he hadn't known he was
holding. At least John was able to feel something.

"Over here, John. Hey, can you hear me?" Keith
had been glad to see John's eyes open, but there was
nothing of the life in them that he had hoped to see.

"Keith—buddy, we didn't make it across the
bridge, did we? I guess you were right, as usual . . . ,"
John began, then coughed with the effort.

"That's enough, John. You stop talking and we'll
take care of you. . . ." Keith stepped away for a
moment as John's eyes closed again and picked up
the patient records from the bed where Denise had
placed them. "He's not oriented to time and place.
We're old buddies, John and I," he explained. "He
was talking about a stunt we pulled when we were
twelve. There was an old bridge that was nothing
more than a couple of ropes and a few slats of wood
here and there. It had been a footbridge sometime in
the thirties, long before the concrete walkway was
put up over the stream. Bill Sonderson and John and
I decided that we were going to be heroes, and
besides, we wanted to prove we weren't afraid of
falling. There was some idiot talk about proving that
we were men. We were halfway across the bridge
when two of the three ropes parted right in the
middle. We all ended up in the hospital with various

bruises, lacerations, and broken bones. It was a good thirty-foot fall directly onto some jagged rocks.''

"But that was years ago?" Denise asked, frowning.

"We were twelve. Let's see, that's twenty-two years in the past."

"I see." Denise's frown deepened. "Why did they send this patient down here? I don't think he's critical, but I also don't think that it's appropriate to send a man with pneumonia and a chest tube down here, no matter how crowded they are on eight!" Denise's cheeks, usually very pale, were splotched with red as her indignation rose.

"Take a look at the drainage from the tube. It's drained more than one hundred twenty milliliters in a little over an hour. What do you make of that?" Keith pointed to the collection chamber.

"I make of it that we have a very sick man here, and someone is going to hear about this transfer. Give me those papers. Who is the doctor who authorized this?"

Denise grabbed the metal file out of Keith's hands and flipped to the bottom of the notes written by the doctor.

"Dr. Shelby. I should have known!" Denise groaned. There was no love lost between the head nurse and Dr. O'Shea's chief resident.

Keith relaxed a little. If Denise was angry, then it meant that he had called this one right on the button. John Alvarez definitely shouldn't be down on the sixth floor.

"Hang in there, old buddy," Keith muttered, and hurried out to the phone to place the page. Within a moment, he heard the voice page over the hospital intercom, and knew that Dr. Shelby's beeper was squawking in her pocket.

Dr. Shelby was unusually prompt in her response

to the sixth-floor call. She came storming up to the desk just as Keith was going back into John's room. She didn't notice that Bill Sonderson was in the room as well.

"What's going on here? I don't even have a minute to sit down and eat without some idiot calling me for no reason at all . . . " she began.

"I think there is a reason," Keith said, and showed her into John's room.

"Oh, it's him," Shelby said, her voice absolutely flat. "Well, I'm glad they finally got him down here. One of the nurses up in Constant Care was making some kind of fuss about it when I wrote out the orders. She doesn't seem to realize that I am the doctor in charge when Dr. O'Shea isn't here."

The message was clear. She had the power and no mere nurse was going to countermand her orders.

"Dr. Shelby, I think you need to take another look at this patient," Denise said quietly. She motioned for the doctor to come forward. "Keith, why don't you tell her what you observed?"

Keith straightened just a little, so that he towered even more above Dr. Shelby. In an instinctively defensive motion, the woman clasped the chart that she had just picked up to her breast.

"He has a temp of one hundred four and a chest tube that has drained more than one hundred twenty milliliters in the last hour. Pupils are slow to respond to light, and he reacts sluggishly to pain stimulus. And he is not oriented to time, place, or date," Keith summed it up quickly.

"So? He was responsive to pain when you finally managed to get his attention, right? He'll come around. And don't worry about that drainage—he's been draining like that for a day, and nothing bad has happened. I had Dr. O'Shea look at him, and he agreed that everything was going fine."

Dr. Shelby started to turn and leave the room, but Denise intercepted her, putting herself between the door and the doctor.

"Dr. Shelby, I want this patient reassigned to the Constant Care Unit. I do not feel that we have the staff or the facilities to take care of a patient in this condition. And while you're at it, I think you'd better call Dr. O'Shea back in here stat for another consultation on this case unless you want a dead patient on your hands!" Denise's voice remained quiet but deadly. There was no time to play games with this half-baked doctor.

"What the hell is all the fuss for? Because a patient has a temp? Lots of them do. Because he had a chest wound caused by a gunshot? Lots of patients come in here with them, most of them straight out of the worst areas of the city. Why won't you listen to me when I tell you I've made a decision on this case and my decision sticks? There wasn't room for the man upstairs—we had another case that needed the bed more. As a matter of fact, the man who took the bed is a friend of my family, and a *very* important man."

She looked at them and blinked rapidly, watching intently to see if they'd caught the point, which was that anyone who knew Dr. Shelby had to be wealthy, important, and therefore deserving of far better care than someone with a permanent natural tan.

"Nevertheless, this transfer at this time is not proper or in the patient's best interest," Denise said stubbornly, unimpressed by Shelby's pretension.

Shelby pursed her lips in exasperation. "Who do you choose to believe about this patient's condition? Me, with all my years of medical school behind me and all my other qualifications, or a male nurse who doesn't know his way around a *cafeteria*, much less know or understand anything about a chest case? He's overreacting, and so are you!"

"Keith and I are in complete agreement. It is absolutely impossible to keep this man here." Denise wasn't about to give in.

Dr. Shelby couldn't believe what she was hearing. "Look, folks, you do whatever you want, but I'm not signing the papers that will move this man back up onto eight. You are perfectly capable of taking care of him here. I'm not about to move my friend out of the Constant Care Unit, when he needs it a lot more than Alvarez does!"

Now Bill Sonderson stepped forward into Shelby's line of vision for the first time.

"Who the hell are *you*?" Shelby demanded irritably.

"My name is Bill Sonderson. I'm a friend of Mr. Alvarez."

"Friends can wait outside. Please leave us alone," Dr. Shelby demanded imperiously.

"I'm also city editor for the *Mercury*. I'd like to have some clarification of some of your comments while you undertook the care of this patient."

Shelby stared at him, her pale eyes bulging slightly. She stiffened and folded her arms even more tightly in front of her.

"I wasn't aware that you were even here," she said nervously. She knew she'd overstepped her bounds, and that she was about to be called on it by someone with far more clout than a couple of nurses.

"As I said, I'd like some clarification. You've just stated that John Alvarez, who is obviously in distress, was transferred from Constant Care because a friend of your family needed the bed more. Does that mean that Ridge is dispensing hospital services on the basis of old family ties instead of need?"

"That wasn't what I meant," Shelby blustered.

"Despite the fact that two experienced nurses are telling you that this patient is in no condition to be on a general-care floor, you are still insisting that he will not be moved back up for more adequate nursing care?"

"I have made that decision, and no one, not even you, is going to make me reverse it!"

"Then could we safely state that because Mr. Alvarez is Hispanic, he cannot expect the same quality of care that will be given to the person who has been brought into the Constant Care Unit to replace him?"

"That's not what I said!"

"But that is what you implied. And unless I get a better explanation from you, that is how it's going to read when a report on this incident is made to the hospital officials and several other interested parties. I wasn't aware that hospitals were allowed to practice discrimination."

"It's *not* discrimination, it's the way life really *is*," Shelby said hotly, then suddenly clamped her mouth shut when she realized what she had just said.

Denise stared at her, aghast at the doctor's words. She couldn't believe that anyone, medical or otherwise, could really feel that way about a patient who had been brought to the hospital for treatment. All patients were equal to Denise. They were all given the best possible care, and they were all given a chance to live, whether they were rich or poor, black, white, or Hispanic. And that was the way it was supposed to be.

"Can I quote you on that?" Bill asked, his voice silky with satisfaction that he had finally goaded her into saying just exactly what he wanted to hear.

Denise smiled in grim satisfaction. This guy wasn't bad, whoever he was. There was no excusing Shelby's attitude or actions, and it looked like Sonderson was about to nail her to the wall.

Sonderson continued, "Tell me, would the chief financial officer of one of the biggest banks in Chicago be 'important,' whether he was Catholic or Jewish, Hispanic or Anglo? Would that person get better treatment than this man has?"

Shelby refused to answer, but it was obvious that the answer was yes.

Bill smiled at her, and Keith thought his friend bore an uncanny resemblance to a shark at that moment.

"Well then, Doctor, this is going to be real interesting to you. Because John Alvarez happens to be the chief financial officer for a very important bank. I'm sure you'd recognize the name—it's the bank that makes certain Ridge Hospital has enough cash to cover your monthly paycheck." Bill's voice was soft. He knew he could make his point without yelling. "Remember, if this man dies, or if he does not get the superb care that everyone knows Ridge can offer each and every patient, you could be in serious trouble. You could, indeed, be in even *more* serious trouble for the attitudes you have expressed here tonight."

"You can't prove a thing!"

"I believe I can. And in the meantime, I think you'd better take care of this patient."

Denise spoke up, her voice still deceptively quiet.

"Dr. Shelby, I am advising you that if John Alvarez isn't transferred out of here immediately and back to

60

Constant Care, and if he isn't given the best care that both you and Dr. O'Shea can provide, I'll make certain that the board knows of both your attitudes *and* your actions."

Shelby's normally thin, pale face had gone stone white, and her big blue eyes had taken on a haunted cast. She hadn't heard a word since Bill had told her who John Alvarez was. How was she supposed to have known that the man was anyone important? If he was such a damned bigwig, why hadn't someone told her about it? Someone must have known. Why hadn't Admitting seen fit to put that information where she could see it and treat him accordingly?

"Transfer him back up, and I'll request further workup," Shelby snapped. She knew when she was whipped. She couldn't do anything about Denise and Keith yet, but she would get back at them in time. She would make Denise Frazier and Keith Jennings pay for this in spades!

The nurse who had transferred the patient down from eight walked into the room just then. She heard Dr. Shelby's words, and looked over at Keith with grudging admiration. She didn't know anything about him, but he had managed to back one of the most pestiferous residents in years into a corner, and she wholeheartedly approved.

"Back to eight?" the nurse asked, and when Shelby nodded, she left to call for the patient transport again as Shelby called after her, "And make it snappy! We need to get to work on him immediately. . . ."

Within minutes John Alvarez had been wheeled out of the room and was on his way back to the Constant Care Unit, Dr. Shelby at his side.

Keith finally managed to get his breathing under control, though he could feel the surge of adrenaline and anger still coursing through him.

"I'm going on up with John, okay?" Bill said, stopping for just a moment. "I want to follow this all the way through. I'll call you later, though, because I need to talk to you." He punched Keith lightly on the shoulder and left the room.

Keith nodded. He was glad to have Bill go with John—there were other patients to be attended to, and work to be done on six. No matter how much he wanted to be with his friend, he couldn't get away at the moment.

"Call me if something happens, all right?" he called after Bill.

"Will do," Bill said as he hurried to catch up with the elevator before it closed.

Keith went back to work, thinking about the various ways in which Bill Sanderson could make something of the incident. With any luck, he concluded, the readers of the *Mercury* would soon know the truth about Shelby and company.

Chapter Five

"Ready to be brought up to date on the new patients?" Patty McDonald asked, and then continued without waiting for Emily's answer. "This has been a weird evening—I swear that ninety percent of the patients are new, and a couple of them are real doozies!" Patty gestured toward the coffeepot in the nurses' lounge and settled down, ready to give Emily all the information she would need for the next shift.

Emily poured herself a cup of very strong, very black coffee. Except in the morning, she tried to stay away from caffeine, but tonight she was definitely going to need it.

"Your shift couldn't have been much worse than my time at home. How come no one ever tells you that there are going to be days when you'll go twenty-four or forty-eight hours without sleep if you have kids?" Emily asked wearily.

Colleen hadn't been feeling well, so Emily had kept her home from school. As a result, Emily had been able to sleep only in snatches. Her daughter didn't really need much care, but Emily couldn't help waking up almost every hour to check on her. Colleen hadn't been terribly sick, just headachy and running a slight temperature. Probably a touch of the flu that was going around.

Emily had fixed her daughter small glasses of orange juice, apple juice, and grape juice, and assorted cookies. It wasn't the most healthful of snacks, but she could sympathize with Colleen when she said she'd rather die than eat nothing but yogurt when she had the flu. She gave in on the food issue and let Colleen watch whatever she wanted on television while Mommy slept. After all, Emily knew that if she had a fever herself, she wouldn't have gone the health-food and public-television-channel route, either.

She had briefed Nora on what had been going on all day when Nora came home from the law office. Nora had tucked both mother and daughter in bed, and had only awakened Emily a couple of minutes before she was due to leave the house. As a consequence, Emily's hair was still slightly damp from her hasty shower, and she wasn't certain she had everything she would need to get through the night. But at least she felt more rested than she had at six in the evening.

"Now, let's see—shall we start with Lara Mendoza? She's quite something, wait until you see her! She's got beautiful black hair, great cheekbones, and tons of gold jewelry—we asked her to send it home, by the way, but she wouldn't do it. Told us she felt naked without it, even for one night. Anyway, she's epileptic, in for her tests. She's been having simple partial seizures about every four hours, no loss of consciousness, but there are sensory symptoms. She experiences heavy sweat and complains of a sharp odor when she recovers from the seizure. She is also extremely lethargic. Right now we've got her on Phenobarb until she's worked up tomorrow.''

Emily noted the name, the drug, and the complaint in her own notebook. Everything was on the chart, but she liked to write it down just to make sure she had everything in her head before she started rounds. She had long ago learned that she might need to consult the notes only once or twice during the week, but it was nice to have them handy just in case. Then she looked up and smiled at Patty.

"Do I detect something more that's not being said?"

Patty smiled wryly. "Just work with her for one night, and I think you'll know what I'm talking about. I won't say anything more—I'd hate to taint your first experience with this woman. But I *will* say that she's got her husband under her thumb. He does everything for her, including helping her to the bathroom, when she really isn't an invalid at all.''

Emily mentally made a note to see this woman soon. Patty was usually an easygoing nurse who let almost everything go past her without much bother. But it was obvious that Lara Mendoza had managed to hit something of a sore spot. Emily knew that most nurses developed those sensitivities after working a couple of years. Some couldn't stand patients who made themselves into invalids when there was no need to be waited on, hand and foot. Others were annoyed by argumentative patients, and for others still, it was the families of the patients who drove them crazy.

"Then we have Tim Thomson—nice guy; he'll be

released tomorrow, I'll bet. He's passing a kidney stone and has had persistent and severe pain. We've got him on pain-killers, with orders written for morphine sulfate if things get really bad. Use your judgment. He's also on IV antibiotics. There was some sign of infection."

Emily made the notation in her notebook—"Tim Thomson, morphine sulfate ordered if pain unrelieved by injections."

"Next?"

"Leopold Peters, back from surgical Constant Care. He had total hip arthroplasty yesterday. Seems that he jogged a little too hard and a little too long, and the joint just shattered."

Emily's eyes sparked with interest. "Good," she muttered. "I hope it hurt like hell!"

Patty stared at Emily, her eyes widening in shock. Emily never said such things, at least not that Patty had ever heard.

"What's that all about?"

"Nothing," Emily said shortly. She wasn't about to go into a detailed explanation of her divorce from Nicholas and her dealings with Leopold Peters.

So good old Leopold Peters was under her care? She wondered how he'd feel when he saw her and realized that the nurse responsible for his injections and his medications and his general care was none other than Nicholas Greer's ex-wife—the same ex-wife whom he had screwed royally during endless court battles over property, alimony, and child support. It should give him quite a turn. Emily smiled slightly in anticipation.

"He's on pain meds and he's already started with the physical therapist. Orders are written for continuing injections through the night, and then tomorrow he's off it and onto pills. He's going to hurt after the therapy, so I imagine he'll take every shot he can get tonight," Patty said.

"That's fine," Emily said. How would good old Leopold react when he realized that she was going to harpoon him in the backside? she wondered. She'd longed to give him a good swift kick there for a long time and now she had a chance to give him something even more painful—the pain meds injections burned like crazy. Oh, she was going to enjoy this!

"That's it for the new patients, and I'm on my way home. Have a good time!" Patty grabbed her coat and breezed out the door without asking the reason for Emily's peculiar response to Leopold Peters.

Emily readied herself to make the rounds to check vitals. She was happy to see that she had managed to leave the house with everything she needed. Thank goodness for the slip-out pocket that allowed her to leave her stethoscope, penlight, and all the other equipment in place, ready to snap right into her uniform.

"Hello, Mrs. Mendoza, I'm Emily Greer and I'll be your nurse tonight. Time for me to check your blood pressure now," Emily said brightly as she hurried into Lara Mendoza's room. She reached for the woman's arm to take her pulse, but Mrs. Mendoza snatched her arm out of Emily's grasp and frowned at her. Her long, heavy, gorgeous earrings shook with the violence of her movements.

"I was just checked, and there's no need to do it again. Why can't you people just leave me alone and let me be sick in peace and quiet? At least when my husband was here, he kept you from bothering me all the time. He takes care of me better than you do," Lara said, her dark eyes flashing. She tapped the padded rails at the side of the bed with one long, blood-red nail, "And you might consider putting these rails down. Look at them—always up, and padded. Someone looking in here would think I was a nut case, and I couldn't stand it if that happened. The previous nurse said that Dr. Barnall had ordered it, but I doubt he would want to *humiliate* me this way."

She looked away. "And as for the tests, all I really need is a little adjustment on the medicine, can't you all see that?"

Emily stared at the woman, momentarily nonplussed by her antagonism. It had been a long time since she'd had a patient who didn't want to be treated or who was so angry about staying overnight in the hospital.

"I'm sorry you feel this way, Mrs. Mendoza, but if Dr. Barnall has decided you need to be here, I certainly wouldn't question him. Now, may I please take your blood pressure and your temperature for your records?" Emily smiled as pleasantly as possible.

Lara sat back against the pillow, her beautiful face looking as if it could have been carved out of stone. She didn't return Emily's smile.

"I don't want to be here. My husband can take care of me, and there's no reason that anyone else needs to know about my problems. And they sure as hell *will* know now that I'm in the hospital for tests and all that other garbage."

Emily nodded. Now she had it pegged. She'd seen this sort of reaction in other patients, particularly patients who suffered from a disease that wasn't quite "socially acceptable." Epileptics were subjected to all kinds of discrimination, including having records of their seizures forwarded to the state medical offices and the department of motor vehicles. The end result for many patients was a deep and not entirely unreasonable distrust of hospitals and doctors. But she still had a job to do, no matter how antagonistic Lara was.

"Damn it . . ." The woman's voice suddenly stopped and her left hand began to jerk uncontrollably, spasming beneath the blood-pressure cuff. Lara was staring off into space, obviously not at all connected with the real world at the moment. It happened so suddenly that it surprised Emily. She took a brief instant to applaud Dr. Barnall's perception. No matter how she felt about it, Lara Mendoza definitely needed to be in the hospital.

Emily draped the stethoscope around her neck and grabbed for the padded tongue blade that Patty had taped to the headboard when Lara was first admitted. Having a tongue depressor readily available was standard procedure with patients who suffered from seizures. Emily was glad the rails were in place—at least the woman couldn't accidentally fall off the side. She might not like it, but it was for her own protection.

Gently Emily worked the blade between Lara's back teeth to keep her from biting her tongue. She was careful to keep her fingers out of the woman's mouth, because lacerated fingers and possible infection weren't something she wanted to deal with at the moment. Emily moved Lara's head to the side, so if she vomited, she wouldn't aspirate the vomitus into her lungs.

She noted that Lara's left leg was now jerking, though not as severely as the hand, and the pupils of her eyes had enlarged as the seizure continued. Then, as abruptly as it started, it was over. Lara closed her eyes and seemed to drift off into a deep sleep.

Emily waited a few more seconds to make certain

that another seizure wasn't going to start and then removed the tongue blade.

"Lara? Lara, can you hear me?" Emily gently tried to awaken the woman. She needed to check her responses and make certain that her patient was back among the living and wasn't going to give a repeat performance within the next few minutes. Luckily this had been a mild seizure, not one of the horrible body-slamming ones that could last up to five minutes and leave both nurse and patient in a state of exhaustion.

"What is it?" Lara fought to open her eyes and finally succeeded. "Is it time for me to go down for the tests?" she asked.

"Nope, you just had a seizure. Nothing big, but I do have to check you out," Emily said. She began to take Lara's pressure again.

Lara lay back, quietly watching the nurse. There was none of the antagonism that had been so noticeable when Emily had first walked into the room. She had almost finished the checks when she noticed a silent trail of tears down Lara's face, and the sight made her ache. She might not like this particular patient, but she could still sympathize with her.

"Well, now you know the worst of it. Damn it, this is so embarrassing . . . " Lara said, her voice barely audible.

"Lara, I'm not certain you'll believe me, but there are a lot worse things than a seizure. You lose a little time, and the people around you might get scared, but it's not that bad."

"The hell it's not!" Lara said, with a flicker of anger in her voice. "It's 'that bad,' when my own mother prays that God will remove the curse from me! And I can't even drive myself to the store because they won't give me a license." She took a deep, trembling breath. "Yeah, it's *that bad*. Try living with something that even your best friends have trouble dealing with."

"It sounds like it must be awfully difficult," Emily agreed. If Lara wanted to talk, she'd given her an opening. Instead, the woman closed her eyes.

"I'm going to sleep now. The seizures always leave me feeling like a limp rag," she said. Then, before Emily could leave, she reached up, took off her elaborate earrings, and handed them to Emily.

"I understand there's a safe where these can be put until my husband can take them home?" she asked, her voice wavering. "Normally I wouldn't be without them—they're kind of a good-luck charm. But I think I can trust you to see that they're carefully taken care of. . . ." Her voice faded and she lay back, almost instantly in a deep sleep.

Emily held the earrings and looked at the sleeping woman. She didn't really have time to put them in the small safe located at the back of the nurses' lounge, but she'd better see about getting them stashed away immediately. She'd ask Denise about the key and combination, and then once they were safe, she'd go on to the next couple of patients.

Oh, that's going to be fun, she thought happily. Leopold Peters at my mercy!

A quick shot of pain-killer for Tim Thomson, another check on Lara Mendoza, vital signs on the other patients, and she was ready for Peters.

"Well, Mr. Peters, and how are *you* tonight? My name, in case you don't remember it, is Emily Greer, the ex-wife of Nicholas Greer, and I'll be your nurse for tonight." She beamed malevolently at him, and was delighted to see him recoil slightly as she walked up to the bed.

Leopold Peters was still as ugly as she remembered. He had a flat nose that had been broken one too many times—probably by outraged ex-wives coming after him with murder in their hearts, she thought gleefully. And then there was the scar on his left cheek that had caught her attention one day. She had asked her own attorney about it, and he had informed her that Peters' second wife had been so mad at him when he came home from one of his all-night parties that she had come after him with a letter opener.

"Now, let me take your blood pressure," Emily crooned, all sweetness and light, wishing that the second wife had managed to aim the blade a little better. About ten inches below the cheek and a bit to the left would have been just fine, if the knife had had an upward thrust. Then Leopold Peters wouldn't have been around to bother anyone at all. Some women, she decided, just didn't have any imagination. Or perhaps it was a case of the woman not wanting to be run in for murder, which Emily thought was a pretty poor excuse when you thought about the world of good that could have been accomplished by removing Leopold Peters from the face of the earth.

Emily's expression normally reflected her sunny disposition, but when Leopold Peters looked at her, all he saw were the emotions that flitted across her face, and he was certain that he saw murder there. A thought belatedly occurred to him—maybe he should have told Nicholas Greer to pay the alimony and child support rather than waiting to see if she'd give up when she ran out of money to pay her attorney. And then there was the matter of paying off the house as agreed in the final papers. He'd let that go an awfully long time, too. Peters' heart began to race as he thought of all the ways, subtle and not so subtle, he had used to make the best possible settlement for his good friend and law partner, Nicholas Greer, and to wipe out any kind of payment to Emily and Colleen. He was only thankful that he hadn't handled any divorces for the doctors involved in his surgery!

He watched her apprehensively as she tightened the blood-pressure cuff, pumping until his arm felt like it would fall off.

"Hey, that's too tight!" he roared.

Emily took the stethoscope out of her ears, and asked him to repeat what he had said, loosening the pressure a little.

"Too tight!" Leopold said gruffly.

"Oh, is that all? It'll be over in just a minute," Emily said, and went back to getting the blood-pressure reading. She had seen on his chart that he was on hypertensive medication, and she could see why. His face was mottled red, and she could feel his heart racing.

So she scared him, did she? He realized that she had him in her power and she could do almost anything to him and no one would know about it. Good! He deserved to twist in the wind for a while. He'd played the same kind of games with the ex-wives of his clients, making them wait for their money and their settlements.

Emily squeezed his toenails, and waited until the pink returned. She noted that there was no swelling of the limbs and that the incision, when she changed the dressing, looked good—no pinkness or swelling. She was certain from the way he flinched each time she touched him that he expected her to pinch his toes with white-hot pliers, or rip off all the tape at one time, taking a goodly amount of hair with it. That might not have been a bad idea, except that the hospital frowned on such techniques.

"How are you feeling, Mr. Peters?" Emily asked pleasantly. "Is that hip giving you any trouble? Do you need anything for the pain? I see that you're almost due for a pain shot."

Peters started to answer, then stopped. He twisted the blanket in his hands, obviously torn between requesting the shot, and telling her to leave him the hell alone. The pain won out.

"I'll take the shot. But I want to see whoever is in charge here, right away!"

"One shot coming right up. And I'll send in Denise Frazier as soon as she's free," Emily agreed.

Good, she thought. Even if Denise listened to Mr. Peters and took her off the case, she'd have given him enough grief to last for a while. She grinned as she thought about the shot coming up.

"Denise, patient in Six forty-one wants to talk to you," Emily sang out as she passed the charge nurse in the hallway.

"Why?"

"Don't know. I imagine it's some complaint or other. He didn't want to talk to me about it," Emily said innocently.

She filled the syringe, capped it, and started back to Mr. Peters' room. She'd give him the shot efficiently and with as little pain as she could, in spite of her animosity. But she hoped he was dreading it, sitting there worrying about what she was going to do to him. Maybe he was thinking about all the times he had lied about Nicholas's assets, until she had pressed her attorney to make a formal complaint, and had given him enough proof to go to the judge. And then there was the alimony that he had all but commanded Nicholas not to pay, even after the court ordered it. After all, his reasoning went, Emily had her own profession. She didn't need any money while she took new classes and got established again after a few years of nursing part-time. She had fought that, too, but she would never forget some of the scathing comments about "money-grubbing little dipshits," as he had so nicely put it in his letters to her own lawyer. Her hands clenched as she thought about that, and then she reminded herself that she was indeed a professional. She might like to act on her feelings, but it was a dead certainty that she wouldn't do it.

She hurried into the room and over to Leopold's bed. He looked at her with stark fear in his eyes, and she showed him the syringe three-quarters filled with milky liquid. She stepped even closer and made quite a production of slipping the sheath off the sharp steel needle.

He took it only so long, and then his nerves got the better of him. "That's okay—I'll do without it, it doesn't hurt that bad. . . ." He tried to scrunch away from her by pulling himself up in the bed.

"Come now, you aren't afraid of a little needle, are you? Here I am, a good, competent nurse, and you seem to expect me to hurt you. Or do you expect some kind of payback for all the needling that you gave *me* while you were handling the case?"

"Look, I'm sorry, I'll get right on it, okay? I'll tell Nicholas he's procrastinated enough." Anything, his eyes pleaded, *anything* at all to make that needle go away.

"Oh, I'm sure you will, if you remember it. But I won't hold out any hope unless I hold that envelope in my hands and the check clears the bank," Emily said, pulling back the sheet.

"Now, turn over on your right side as far as you

can, and I'll just slip this in." She briskly exposed his rear end, and swabbed with a cold alcohol prep pad.

"*Ohhhh . . .*," Peters moaned. Even the prep seemed to have little barbs attached.

"Here we go!" Emily caroled, and jabbed the needle in. She didn't even give it the extra push she would have loved to deliver. She just squeezed down on the plunger and the pain-killer burned its way into the muscle. If she couldn't give him pain herself, then she'd let the medicine do the work for her.

"*Ow*! Oh, damn! Ouch!" Peters whined. Suddenly his Ivac began to beep.

"What's going on with that thing, I wonder?" Emily said as she removed the needle and went over to the disposal unit that was in every room. She dropped the needle into the bright red container, then hurried over to the beeping machine and pushed the button that made the infernal sound stop. She checked the tubing and the bag, noting no difficulty, until she reached the IV site on the inside of his elbow. Even under the tape, the skin looked swollen and red, and she could see droplets of IV fluid seeping out from underneath the patch.

"Well, it looks like we have a problem—the IV seems to have infiltrated. That means we have to move it to another location because the medicine you need can't pass through into the vein. Time to start another one, because we can't take you off these fluids quite yet," Emily explained cheerfully.

Peters' normally ruddy complexion had faded from bright red to dusky red to parchment white. His broad, flat face was now almost as colorless as his gray hair. He seemed to gulp between every other word, a sure sign of nerves frayed almost to the breaking point.

"I hate hospitals, I hate doctors, and I hate nurses,

but most of all I hate needles," he said, and there wasn't even a trace of the grand, booming voice that filled the courtroom when he was engaging in the theatrics of his profession.

"Sorry about that, but I have to do this."

"I could refuse. I could check myself out. You don't have a right to keep me here against my will!" He was beginning to regain a little of his bluster.

"Yes, you could check yourself out. But you'd have to sign all kinds of releases absolving the hospital and the doctors from any charges if things went bad. And then, of course, you wouldn't find anyone here to help you. That cast is pretty unwieldy to try and handle all on your lonesome," Emily said.

Peters knew when he was beaten. "Fine, go ahead and start the IV if you have to. But I'd prefer to have another nurse do it."

"There aren't any available. They've all got their own patients to take care of," Emily said as she set up the kit for reestablishing the IV.

Surprisingly, he had good veins, and Emily was sad to discover that starting the drip again was going to be relatively easy.

"Little prick," Emily chirped, relishing the double meaning. Peters, however, took one look at the thin, flexible plastic tubing that was going to be inserted into his arm and promptly leaned back against the pillow with his eyes closed. It wasn't quite a faint, but it was close enough. By the time he could face the world again, the whole procedure was over and the IV monitor was merrily flashing green again.

Emily had finished and was leaving the room just in time to collide with Denise as the charge nurse came into the room in response to Peters's request. Emily stood outside the open door, shamelessly eavesdropping on the conversation.

"Look, I want a different nurse. I'll pay more, I just want a different one, all right?" Mr. Peters said.

Emily heard Denise's murmured response, but couldn't make out the words.

"I don't *care* about work loads! I don't *care* about what the policy is! I just want *another nurse*!" Peters was beginning to bellow, and Emily knew very well that Denise never gave in to people who yelled at her.

"Fine, Mr. Peters, I will see what is available. However, it might be the end of the shift before we can even begin to work on your request," Denise said as she left his bedside.

Denise and Emily headed back to the desk together, waiting until they were well out of earshot before discussing the situation.

"The question becomes, do you want to keep him as a patient, or would you rather trade with someone else? He seems to be rather difficult to get along with," Denise said as she studied Peters' chart.

"No problem. I don't mind him, and there really isn't anyone I'd want to trade with. Why upset the schedule now?" Emily said sweetly, the perfect angel of mercy.

"All right, if you don't object. But watch out for him—he makes me think of a man who isn't hinged quite tight enough," Denise said as she closed the file with a snap.

"Don't worry, I can take care of him," Emily assured her. Fate had finally given her a break. She intended to enjoy every minute of taking care of Leopold Peters.

Chapter Six

"Hey, Johnny, how the hell you doing?" Bill Sonderson leaned over the bed in the Constant Care Unit and looked at his friend. There were still tubes everywhere, but John's color was good, and his eyes were bright and alert. He looked a lot better than he had the last time Bill had seen him two days ago.

Keith heaved a sigh of relief as he looked at the monitors and grabbed an arm to take a quick pulse, even though John wasn't a patient of his. He was obviously awake and alert, and Keith was glad to see that the chamber from the chest tube held only a minor amount of fluid, in contrast to the 120 milliliters that had been present a few days before. In fact, two days earlier, he wouldn't have given any kind of prognosis for this kind of recovery.

"Did you get the number of the bullet that hit me?" John said, his voice weak and thready. It still hurt to take a full breath, even though the nurses had him coughing almost every fifteen minutes to clear out his chest and to make sure that once the pneumonia was gone, it stayed gone.

"They tell me that tomorrow the chest tube will be out, but I'll believe it when I see it," he added. He was acutely conscious of the feeling of the tube going through his skin and into the lung. There were times when he had to grab onto the bars to keep from pulling the tube out himself because it was such an irritation. The skin around the tube was blotched and red. The nurses had already been in twice today, and Dr. Shelby once to fix it so that it wasn't leaking from deep inside him.

Keith moved aside so Bill could step up to John's bed.

John grasped his friend's hand, squeezing it three times in quick succession, the old club signal that they'd worked out for trouble ahead. He was glad to see Bill Sonderson, and even more glad that his friend was a newspaperman. He'd been trying to find out exactly what had happened to him when that shot had blasted through the plate-glass window, but no one could or would tell him anything about the investigation. The cops had come and gone and told him nothing. The nurses acted like they didn't even know he'd been shot. But Bill would know everything about this case, stuff that even some of the city investigators wouldn't know. Bill had always been a snoop, and his newspaperman instincts came out even more strongly when one of his friends was concerned. He'd find out what had really happened at the restaurant.

"Have they got the bastards who did this?" John demanded. He'd lain there, drifting in and out of sleep, racked by pain, and silently determined that if he had a chance, he'd kill the son of a bitch who had shot him almost point blank. He was lucky he wasn't dead instead of just wounded.

"Not a clue, John. I hate to tell you, but the police have almost shelved it. After all, the only person who was killed in the shoot-out was another crack dealer, and the cops aren't going to worry too much about that. You survived, and besides, there weren't any witnesses. Imagine that—on a crowded street in the middle of a good section of town, there were no reliable eyewitnesses," Bill said sarcastically.

"I can tell them what he looked like. I had one hell of a good look right before he aimed the gun at the man who was standing on the street in front of the window. The first blast meant for that other guy happened to hit me instead. . . ." John tried to sit up, and all his monitors suddenly started beeping. "Just give me a chance to ID him, okay?"

"Mr. Alvarez, stop it this minute!" The nurse came rushing over at the cacophony of the various monitors recording his outburst. "Don't get yourself in an uproar. If this is what your friends' visit is going to do to you, then we're going to bar them until you're back down on a general-care floor," she said in her Number One stern voice. Keith, however, was a fellow nurse, so she didn't mind having him around on his breaks or during lunch. "You'll have to settle down, or everyone except Keith will have to leave. Can't throw *him* out—after all, he's responsible for you being alive." The Constant Care charge nurse reset the machines that monitored John's respiratory rate, his heart rate, and his IV rate. Personally, she didn't think he needed all of them anymore, but Dr. Shelby had been absolutely insistent that John Alvarez was to get the best treatment possible.

"What does she mean, Keith?" John looked up at his friend, who had been standing back a bit so John and Bill could talk.

"Oh, nothing. At least nothing I'm going to tell you about here and now. But I expect our resident journalist is going to make something nice and juicy out of this." Keith didn't dare say anything more. He was acutely aware of the charge nurse listening to everything that was said. And besides, John didn't need to know about his original treatment at Ridge. He would find out later, when he'd had a chance to recuperate and was strong enough to stand the fury that he would probably feel when he discovered how he had been shunted aside.

Keith and Bill visited with John for a few more minutes. Both men were silent as Keith walked Bill to his car.

"Okay," Bill said, "it's time to talk over tactics. I played the tape I made that night when Shelby was giving you so much trouble. Everyone who was in the conference thought it might be the beginning of one hell of a good story. But I'm going to need your help."

"Anything you want, Bill," Keith replied. He'd hoped that John would think what was happening at Ridge would be worth pursuing. Because if what he heard was true, Dr. Shelby wasn't the only physician at Ridge who needed to be called to account.

"I need help in putting this together, and you're on the inside. We've come up with what could be a dynamite series of investigative pieces about the city's private hospitals, beginning with Ridge. I can see the headlines now—'Rich Ridge—Only the Wealthy Receive Adequate Care!' A whole series about how each hospital treats patients when they're brought into the Emergency Room. Do they wait until they've found out about insurance before they start treatment? Do they just refuse to admit uninsured patients and ship them off to the local county hospital? The next article in the series will deal with what happens to those patients if they make it through the first part of the gauntlet and then are admitted to the hospital."

"You need contacts then, people who will be willing to give interviews?"

"Actually, I was thinking more along the lines of having people give me a call when a patient comes in who might be at risk. If they're not getting adequate care, if they've been shunted aside, I can come in and talk to the patient, and then, if it's all right, I'll stay and listen to how the doctors react to these patients. We've already got a couple of doctors who are willing to review cases to make certain we're not being taken in when a situation looks serious and it really isn't."

Keith smiled. "You've got it, Bill. That's just the kind of thing I was hoping you'd come up with," he said gratefully. "This whole problem has me really bothered. I can't believe that most of the staff would have treated John Alvarez so badly. It has to be isolated pockets of trouble, not the whole hospital."

Keith leaned against the car, his hands deep in his pockets, his shoulders hunched as if he were expecting to ward off blows from an unseen assailant. And blows, he knew, would come if his part in the investigation were ever uncovered. Ridge administration didn't like troublemakers.

"The thing that bothers me is the assumption that no one who isn't lily white is going to have insurance enough to pay for a sudden, catastrophic trauma," Keith went on. "Look at John—if he hadn't been having dinner with the president of the bank, the paramedics might have decided to take him to County instead of Ridge, and that's a good fifteen minutes further away. John was unstable and in deep distress when he was wheeled into Ridge's emergency room."

Keith had read the transcripts of the information given by the paramedics as they headed for Ridge Emergency. It was a miracle that John hadn't died right in the middle of the restaurant. They had reported a sucking sound from John's chest, a sure sign that the bullet had punctured a lung. It was only by the paramedics' quick action that John had been kept from going into complete respiratory failure.

Keith continued, "If the president hadn't been right behind the ambulance, and hadn't signed John in, showed insurance forms and such, John still might have been refused treatment and dumped on another hospital. It's against the rules, of course—no one is supposed to do that with any patient who isn't stabilized and able to be transported, but it happens."

"I know," Bill agreed. "That's why this series is going to go far beyond patient-dumping. From your explanation of what happened night before last, there was a good chance that John might have died if you hadn't forced the doctor to treat him. We want to expose the doctors who make these decisions. They've been able to cover their tracks in the past, but this time we're going to nail them. If they discriminate against patients of different ethnic backgrounds, the hospital and those doctors must answer for their attitudes."

Keith had been thinking of one problem, and it was time to talk about it.

"Do you have to tell everyone that you're a newspaper reporter? Couldn't you just go in undercover, like a cleaning man or something? I'm afraid the minute they know who you are, the doctors are going to clam up."

"Sometimes that happens, of course. But you'd be surprised what people will say, even in front of a reporter. And yes, I do have to announce it," Bill said. "I'm looking forward to the possibility of a Pulitzer with this series. I couldn't win if I didn't follow the rules, and one of the rules is never to trick a source. Always tell the person that you work for a newspaper. That way they can't claim they'd been lied to."

"Pulitzer material? Come on, Bill, it isn't that big a story!"

"Yes, it is. Patient care all over the U.S. is suffering from exactly the same troubles that affect the patients in Ridge. It's a good, solid story and I'm going to make it work."

"What do you need from me?"

"Like I said, contacts. Find me nurses who will call me when there's a problem. Find doctors who don't like what's going on. Make certain they'll call me if there's trouble. That's what I need."

Bill looked at his watch and whistled in surprise. "I'm going to be late for a meeting if I don't hurry up. Listen, I've got to go. Just remember, I need leads, I need information, I need to be in the right place at the right time."

"I'll do it," Keith promised.

"And don't worry, we'll make certain they can't ever trace it back to you, so your job won't be in jeopardy," Bill promised.

"Doesn't matter if it *is* in jeopardy. Go ahead and use my name if you want. I have another offer that's looking better and better with each passing day. I'd like to be working in a facility that deals with brain-damaged adults, helping them come back to leading a normal life. Ridge may not have the use of my talents for much longer."

Bill nodded and closed the window. Keith stood on the curb while he watched the car leaving the parking lot. It was almost time to start his shift, but he hesitated a few moments, sorting through the conversation of the past few minutes.

The easiest way to help Bill would be to find some incident of discrimination in process, and then call Bill and tell him to come to the hospital immediately. Bill would have to think of a way to insinuate himself into the situation, but if anyone could carry off the assignment, he could. Once he started asking questions and getting answers, Bill would have his story. And once the staff was alerted to media attention, lives could be saved. Eyewitness reports would certainly be interesting, and Ridge and the doctors would be hard pressed to say that the incidents never happened.

"Damn, I've got to talk to Suzi," Keith said, snapping his fingers as he remembered a conversation with an attractive black nurse on the Ob Gyn floor. He had heard her complaining about the treatment given to low-income women who came to Ridge to have their babies. She had told him that because of the high-risk factors involved, Ridge was considering closing the Ob Gyn floor to anyone who was not a patient of one of the staff doctors. That would assure them of some kind of protection against suit if something went wrong.

Keith caught Suzi right before she checked in.

"Suzi, can you take just a minute? I need your help."

Suzi's face lit up. She liked Keith. Given the chance, she would have encouraged him to get to know her better, but as yet he hadn't shown much interest in her as a woman, only as a nurse.

"Remember our discussion about discrimination? The ways doctors can give bad care to minorities and low-income people without being called to account?" Keith asked, when he was certain they were out of earshot of the other nurses. It was risky talking like this within the hospital, but he didn't know when he'd have time to meet Suzi outside and explain what Bill was going to attempt to accomplish.

"Yeah—had a case last night, as a matter of fact," Suzi said. "A woman came in in labor, and it was obvious that there was fetal distress. They picked it up downstairs. She should have been taken in for a C section. Instead, the doctor stuck her on monitors and left her in the hallway for forty-five minutes, with no one really in charge. When she was finally taken into the OR it was too late for the baby. This doctor is a real loser. He has a history of ignoring black patients, whether they're paying customers or not. Same Doc doesn't like black nurses and makes snide comments about our competence every time he has a chance."

"If things like that are happening, you've got to help me," Keith said, and explained Bill's plan as briefly as he could.

"Here's the phone number. Call him at any time, when something is happening in the hospital. With Bill on the scene, we'll have an eyewitness. And we might just cause some doctors to attempt to give better care. Remember, too, it's not Ridge that's on trial, it's those doctors and a few of the nurses, too, who think that rich is right, and that the poor deserve no care at all."

Suzi took the hastily scrawled number and stuck it

in the pocket of her uniform. She'd call all right. There were too many instances of abuse going on to let the attitudes of Dr. O'Shea, Dr. Shelby, and others continue.

"Count on me—and I'm going to be late if I don't go in right now!" Suzi said as she hurried toward the nurses' station.

Keith was in a fine mood as he rode the elevator down to his own floor and clocked in, ready to begin his own round of work. He'd have Coralie Cooper again tonight, and he was hoping the old lady was better than she had been the past couple of days. Massive doses of corticosteroids had managed to lessen the inflammation in her joints and ease the pain of the arthritis attack, but the relief was temporary. She would need long-term therapy. Coralie was strong and determined to walk and work in her beloved garden again, but it would be a long struggle.

Keith knew it was bad nursing practice, but he had become attached to Mrs. Cooper. She was spunky, a real fighter, and even when she hurt so bad most people would have been crying, she never let it get her down.

Coralie looked up and smiled when Keith came into the room.

"My, I'm glad to see your face, Keith! I've been looking over the seed catalogues again, and I think I'm about ready to try some new things this year. Can you imagine, I'm going to grow loofah sponges and give everyone I know a grand expensive bath sponge for Christmas. I've given everyone so many pickles and spiced apples and other stuff that I'm sure they're sick of it. But scrubbing sponges, *that's* something altogether different," Coralie said a little too heartily. She sounded much better, though she was still pale.

"Loofahs sound great to me. I use them in the bath

all the time, and they're terrific for scrubbing an itchy back. The people on your gift list should like it just fine. Speaking of which, I noticed here that you didn't take a bath this morning—what happened? And this can't be true—they're saying that you haven't been out of bed once, not even to go to the bathroom?"

Coralie lost what color there was in her cheeks. She pulled back as he touched her arm to take her pulse.

"I'm fine, really I am," she said.

"Well, did they at least change your bed?" he asked, exasperated at whoever had been on the morning shift and hadn't written up any deviation from the schedule.

"No, not that, either . . ."

Coralie looked at Keith for a minute, and suddenly her face crumpled; tears began to run in rivulets down the wrinkles in her cheeks.

"Please help me, Keith. I have to go to the bathroom, and I can't . . . I can't walk."

"Coralie!" Keith was instantly beside her, patting her shaking shoulder.

"What is it? Why can't you get up? Do you need the bedside commode?"

Coralie just sobbed harder and shook her head.

"I can't even use that—oh please, give me a bedpan!"

Keith snatched open the door of the small bedside stand and took out the plastic bedpan that came in every patient's admissions kit.

"Here, let me slip this under you." Keith lifted the old woman gently, working her blue nightgown above her hips.

Coralie sobbed even harder, then didn't make any sound as she tried to bite back a scream of pain.

Keith drew the curtains around the bed. He should

have done that first, but from the look on Coralie's face, she couldn't have waited another second.

"All through?" he asked a few minutes later.

Coralie nodded, and Keith disposed of everything and hurried back.

"Now, tell me what this is all about."

Coralie looked down, as if she couldn't bring herself to say anything.

"Look, either tell me, or I'll have your doctor come in. I don't care which it is, but you can't just hide how you're feeling from us. That's dangerous!"

Silently Keith cursed the uncaring nurse who had not responded to the woman's obvious distress during the day shift. Could side effects of the medication Coralie was taking be causing her trouble? Could she have lost control of her legs? He didn't remember ever hearing about a side effect like that, but it might be mentioned in the *Physician's Desk Reference* at the nurses' station. Or had something gone wrong with her kidneys and her back hurt too much for her to be able to move?

"I think I broke my leg," Coralie finally said, barely making herself heard.

Keith groaned inwardly. God! She'd broken her leg and he'd moved her? He'd lifted her onto the bedpan and down off it again, her legs had shifted, and she hadn't told him? How was he going to explain complications of a fracture which had been caused by his handling of her?

"Which leg?" Keith asked, trying to keep his voice under control so he didn't panic her any more than she already was.

"The right one," Coralie sniffed. She pulled the blanket back so he could see her legs.

Keith looked down and winced at what he saw. Her

90

right leg, about six inches below the kneecap, was badly bruised and swollen. Worse, the bone was obviously offset. Even though the end wasn't protruding through the skin, it was a very bad break.

"Coralie, how did this happen?"

"I don't know," the woman whispered.

Keith looked at her. She was lying, he knew she was, but he couldn't imagine why since she was in dreadful pain and had been all day, from the looks of it.

"Coralie, I'm going to have to check your chest right away, okay? Nothing to be worried about," he said, lying mightily himself. He moved her forward slightly and listened to her lungs as Coralie wiped away the tears that still flowed freely. Everything sounded clear.

Keith was now ready to continue the check of her lungs. He pulled the top buttons of her nightgown apart, exposing the flesh around her neck and upper chest. He was looking for tiny, perfectly round spots that would signify that they were dealing not only with a break, but with a potentially fatal fat embolism. He heaved a sigh of relief when he saw no discoloration.

"I'm going to call Dr. Mendelsohn right now. Don't move, don't do *anything*, because this is serious," Keith instructed her.

He left Coralie to go out to the phone at the nurses' station, explain the disaster to Denise Frazier, and call the doctor. He described the state of the leg, including the swelling, discoloration, and the obviously offset bone, and mentioned that he had already checked for the rash that would have indicated a fat embolism.

"That's fine. I'll be right over. Keep her immobilized, as I'm certain you already know. Stupid of me to say it, Keith—you're a good nurse," Dr. Mendelsohn said and hung up the phone.

Keith was glad that if Coralie had to have something go wrong, it was Dr. Mendelsohn who would be taking care of her. He lived only fifteen minutes from the hospital, so if there was an emergency, he could always get there right away. He could have asked his chief resident to take the call—it was almost midnight—but he had never in his life passed on the responsibility for a hard case, and Coralie Cooper was definitely that.

Within the half hour, Coralie had been taken down to X ray. Dr. Mendelsohn was ready for surgery, and soon Coralie was sporting a cast that could be gotten wet and then dried with a blower. She particularly needed that type of cast, since hydrotherapy was still a daily event to ease the pain of her arthritis attack.

Dr. Mendelsohn went up to the sixth floor and found Keith.

"She'll be back down in about six hours, and I imagine this will lengthen her stay a couple of days—maybe even a week, depending on how soon her bones start to heal. The bad thing about it is her age added to the degenerative bone disease and loss of calcium. Wish there was a way I could wave a magic wand or make a magic potion and have every bone in the world be as strong as possible—knock out all this damn osteoporosis and brittle bones and the rest of it. Of course, I'd put myself out of business, but that would be all right," the doctor said as he gave Keith the report on Coralie. "But the reason I really came back up here is to find out how this happened."

Keith shrugged. "I wish I could help you. I saw she hadn't voided since early this morning, and she hadn't been given a bath or had her bed made. That riled me, especially since she was practically crying for a bedpan. So I gave her one." Keith looked at Mendelsohn and shook his head miserably. "I may have made the break worse than it was. She hadn't told me there was a problem, so I wasn't careful enough. I wasn't thinking of a broken leg. I wondered if there was some side effect of the drugs she'd been receiving that I didn't know about. Then I just wondered if the nurses on the other shift had been careless."

"Don't worry, you didn't cause any damage. The damage was done when she broke the bone. But there are no reports of a slip and fall? She didn't take a tumble moving in and out of bed?"

"Not that I know of. From the nursing reports, she didn't move all day."

The doctor ran his hand over his face in frustration. Coralie had been in too much pain to tell him how the break had occurred, and when the medication finally lessened the pain, she had fallen asleep from sheer exhaustion.

"I guess we'll just have to wait until Coralie can tell us, then, won't we?"

Dr. Mendelsohn went back down to check on his patient once more before he left Ridge. There was something about this whole episode that bothered him. Coralie had been an unfailingly cheerful, responsive patient, even through the worst of her attacks. She had been willing to try anything and rarely complained, even if the treatment was unpleasant. In fact, the physical therapist had noted in the chart that she had warned Coralie about overexerting. Several mentions were made of her desire to get back to her home and her garden. Her daughter-in-law and grandson, he remembered, were supposed to be taking care of things, but she doubted their competence with a hoe.

It would have to wait. Coralie would tell them eventually how the break had happened. She'd have to, because they had to know if the hospital had been at fault in any way. . . .

Chapter Seven

"This nurse was responsible for that fire, and for the death of Mr. Harper. That should be clearly noted, and a report should be forwarded not only to the nursing administration but possibly even to the State Board of Nursing," Dr. O'Shea said, his voice loud in the room.

George Evans, the counsel for the hospital, who was asking questions about the fire, tightened his grasp on the pen he was holding. This doctor, he decided, was a major pain. If the man continued to make himself obnoxious, he was going to be asked to leave. The story of what had really happened the night Mr. Harper had died would never be told if Dr. O'Shea continued his persecution of Emily Greer.

"Now, Dr. O'Shea, this is just an inquiry into what happened," he said calmly. "We're not attempting to pin the blame on anyone, so I'd appreciate it if you would refrain in the future from making such statements. Imagine the damage to the hospital's reputation, particularly if your analysis of the situation proves to be incorrect."

Evans was beginning to lose his patience. O'Shea had been ranting on for almost forty-five minutes, blocking any real progress on discussing the incident report with Emily Greer. He was beginning to wonder if O'Shea was on something—a normal man didn't reveal that kind of unreasoning hatred for anyone, not even a nurse with whom he disagreed. It wouldn't have been the first time in medical history that a doctor had tried to cover up his addiction either to some kind of drugs or to alcohol. One of the clearest signs of that kind of compensation was blaming others for his own mistakes or oversights. If O'Shea continued to obstruct the inquiry, Evans was going to report the good doctor to the board of trustees as a person who would bear watching in the future.

George Evans was careful about making such accusations. It wouldn't be a formal report, actually nothing more than a mention of his actions. It would perhaps be given over dinner, while they were all enjoying good wine and fine food. He could just let it slip that O'Shea seemed to be on edge and very argumentative. Certainly Evans could state that O'Shea's judgment didn't seem to be as acute as it had been in the past. The men and women of the board would listen. They had listened before about other problems concerning doctors who had subsequently been eased out of the hospital or sent to a clinic or other rehabilitation facilities to cure their addictions.

Now Emily was motioned to continue with her report.

"Mr. Harper had been a patient in the hospital for several days and was admitted with a diagnosis of status asthmaticus—that means he was having an asthma attack which wasn't responding to the normal therapy," Emily added when she saw the puzzled look on Evans's face. Then she continued, "During that time, it was noted in his chart that even in the midst of severe asthma attacks, he would continue to smoke. He was receiving heavy medication to keep his lungs clear and air moving, yet he thwarted all efforts of the staff to keep him from lighting a cigarette. Nurses reported finding him smoking in the bathroom with the door locked, smoking in bed with the oxygen disconnected—and this was a man who was dependent on that oxygen. He would go down to the solarium at meal times so he could smoke when no one was watching."

"Are you saying that this pattern of compulsive smoking caused the fire?" Evans asked, frowning. The late Mr. Harper sounded like a nut case. What kind of man would come into a hospital for treatment of a severe breathing disorder and still sneak cigarettes?

O'Shea stood up then and slapped the long pine table for emphasis.

"Oh, for God's sake, will you stop trying to get her to say that it was Mr. Harper's fault that there was a fire? It wasn't anything of the sort! Emily Greer is just a lousy nurse who didn't watch out for her patients. She's been a bad nurse for years. She simply was unable to control Mr. Harper."

Dr. O'Shea was ticking off Emily's offenses on his fingers. "She didn't know how to handle the emergency when it happened. She didn't watch the patient. She didn't exercise necessary caution. She was slow in responding. I've seen reports that say the fire was still going two and a half minutes later when the fire fighters arrived on the scene. Now, does that sound like this woman is competent?"

"That's it, Dr. O'Shea! I warned you about your outbursts. Leave this room immediately!" Evans stood up and glowered at this man who was obstructing every attempt to unravel what had actually happened. Evans wasn't interested in laying blame and he wasn't interested in explanations. He just wanted to make certain that the hospital wouldn't be hurt if there were an investigation, or, God forbid, a lawsuit filed in the case.

"You can't make me leave, Evans! I'm not going to allow you to whitewash the idiocy of this woman. Why don't you ask her how many of her patients have died because she didn't watch them closely enough? If she had responded to Harper's smoking in the first place, this whole mess wouldn't have happened!"

The counsel smiled, and O'Shea noted uncomfortably that it wasn't a friendly smile.

"By 'respond,' do you mean control him? Oversee him? Is that what you're saying? In other words, Dr. O'Shea, you *knew* about the man's habit of smoking. I presume that you had warned him of the dangers?"

"I warned him about smoking, but I didn't warn him that he would be burned to death because a nurse didn't get there in time to shut off the oxygen!" O'Shea was wavering a bit now. Even after a few drinks, he was smart enough to know that if a patient was intent upon killing himself with cigarettes or whatever other means were at hand, there wasn't a doctor or nurse in any hospital who could stop him from doing so.

"In other words, you expected the nurses to act as bloodhounds, keeping their noses on alert for any signs that a patient with a chronic lung disease was again smoking in his room? You wanted them to be policewomen for a fifty-five-year-old man who had been warned repeatedly that not only was smoking bad for his health during an asthma attack, but who had also been informed about the volatile materials in hospital rooms?" Evans shook his head angrily. "Why the hell should they have baby-sat this man if he was such a damned fool? Didn't Mr. Harper have some personal responsibility for his actions?" Evans was shouting now, nose to nose with O'Shea.

O'Shea backed away. He blinked, then stared down at the table.

Evans was satisfied. He'd finally managed to get through to O'Shea. And there was another by-product of the face-to-face confrontation. He now knew for certain that the doctor apparently had consumed a lot of bourbon. Even with breath freshener, the smell came through. A drinker, and already far gone at nine in the morning. Superstar thoracic surgeon or not, the board would have to be told. They couldn't tolerate any scandal or even a hint of trouble—their insurance was already too high as it was.

He continued, "It's my responsibility to protect this hospital from a lawsuit that could be filed by someone who thinks, as you do, that Mr. Harper should have been watched like a naughty child to keep him from doing harm to himself either by smoking while having an attack, or as it turned out, from blowing himself to hell. Now, I suggest you leave, Dr. O'Shea. You are obstructing me in the performance of my job, and I tend to have a very short temper and a wild left hook when that happens!"

O'Shea glared at the attorney, making plans of his own to take his case to the board of trustees and the rest of the administration. He wouldn't rest until Evans was removed as hospital counsel. No one could be allowed to threaten Dr. Milton O'Shea. *No one*, not for any reason!

Evans ignored the anger on O'Shea's face. He didn't have time for prima donnas. If O'Shea had him fired, he'd be delighted. He was already beginning to regret having taken the position in the hospital. He would have been far better off in his own small private practice, without the aggravation of doctors who seemed in all too many cases to consider themselves only slightly less important than God.

"Mrs. Greer, why don't you describe what happened that night, when you walked into Mr. Harper's room? I'm certain Dr. O'Shea won't interrupt you again—if he decides to stay."

Emily began to give the information, describing how she and Nurse Richards had both smelled smoke. By the time Emily had isolated the source of the smoke as Martin Harper's room, he was puffing away with the oxygen cannula still attached. She had not been able to reach him before the oxygen exploded.

"See, she killed him! She should have been more aware of what was going on. She should have reached him earlier. I don't understand why she didn't turn off the oxygen at the desk the instant she smelled the smoke!" Dr. O'Shea was on his feet again, bellowing at Emily.

Emily threw up her hands in exasperation. "And leave the heart patients without oxygen? What about the other people dependent upon it? Yes, I *could* have done that, but if I had, and Mr. Harper or other patients had been adversely affected, I'd *still* be in trouble!"

Dr. O'Shea's beeper cut off Emily's declaration.

"I'll be back. Don't you do anything until I return!" he thundered as he strode out of the room.

Within ten minutes, all the evidence that needed to be gathered had been recorded. Evans was delighted to fold up his papers, put them in his briefcase, and snap the locks. It was still early morning, but after dealing with Dr. O'Shea, he felt the need for a stiff bourbon himself. A Perrier, however, would have to suffice. "Don't worry about it," he told Emily. "The hospital can't be held liable for a patient's stupidity. We just need a clear record of what actually happened so if Harper's family decides to file a suit, we have all the answers on hand."

Emily nodded. She didn't care what they did with the information, as long as O'Shea stayed off her back. What she really needed to do was go home and get some sleep. Colleen was back in school, and that left the whole glorious day to sleep and recoup before her next shift.

Emily walked out of the room and down the hallway, looking around and hoping that she wouldn't run into O'Shea or Shelby. She dreaded even seeing them. She dreaded being assigned their cases, and more than anything, she dreaded the thought of working in this hospital for years to come, with Dr. O'Shea harassing her until he finally decided to retire. She knew there wasn't a chance that he'd leave her alone. She remembered hearing something about another nurse who had been the object of O'Shea's attacks for almost four years, until she finally left. It seemed that the great thoracic surgeon never gave up—he just drove the people he didn't like out of the hospital, not caring who was hurt in the process. Emily knew she was going to be next in line. She would be better off finding another job, away from Ridge and Dr. O'Shea.

"Emily, have you got a minute?"

Emily jumped at the male voice. It took her a moment to realize that it wasn't Dr. O'Shea.

She turned and saw Dr. Terry Barnall coming toward her at his usual lope, his stethoscope bouncing with every step. Even though he looked tired, he still did everything at a run, as if there wasn't enough time in the day to get all his work done.

"Hi, Terry, how's it going this morning?" Emily asked. She knew that Dr. Barnall usually started surgery at six in the morning, and there were some days when he wasn't finished until four or five in the afternoon. Today was a surgery day, she was almost certain.

"Light day. Can't imagine what happened to all the neurosurgical problems we usually seem to have. I expected at least five shunts, a bunch of tumors—you know, the general run of business for a Thursday. We should have been up in OR for hours yet, but we ran out of patients. Most likely they'll hit Emergency tonight in a pack, all of them demanding that we operate immediately." Barnall grinned at her, his whole face lighting up animatedly. "I have a theory about it, you know. I think the full moon stimulates the brain and increases the production of cerebrospinal fluid, which consequently increases the pressure within the brain, and then all the problems that were dormant pop up and present themselves for us to fix. It happens like clockwork every damn time the moon is full, so obviously there's a correlation."

Emily laughed at the ridiculous suggestion. "Yes, well, the theory sounds fine, but somehow I don't think you should present it to the chief of staff quite yet, do you?"

"Nah, I'll wait until I'm out of this nut house and

write a paper on it. I should win a Nobel Prize, at least."

They reached the elevator, and Emily pushed the down button.

"Where are we going, by the way?" Dr. Barnall asked innocently.

"I don't know where *you're* going, but *I* have to go home, take a bath, eat, and then fall into bed. I had to come in this morning and tell the house counsel all about that horrible fire. Every time I go past that room, I still can smell burning flesh and hear the roaring of flames."

"That was a pretty bad scene, I know. I was there right after the fire, and it was a mess," Dr. Barnall said. "I heard something about Shelby jumping you the other day about it—something about her thinking that you were at fault, which is just plain stupid."

Emily was about to correct him, but he hurried on. "Don't let her get to you. That woman is never going to make it as a physician if she doesn't change the way she acts toward patients and staff. Do you know, the other day she had a patient who was waiting for results from a mammography study, and she just walked into the woman's room, told her that she had cancer and that it looked inoperable. Then, boom, she walked out the door. We had to restrain the woman, get someone in to talk to her, and then call Shelby back in to explain just what this woman had to look forward to, and to emphasize that despite Shelby's statements, she still had a chance of survival."

"Did she act more professional the second time around?" Emily asked.

"She did—after a small warning from me. I caught her outside the patient's door and escorted her down to the end of the corridor. I promised her that if she wasn't kind and compassionate, two things that were utterly foreign to her nature, she was going to be mangled six ways from Sunday the next time she decided to run in the same race with me. We're both into running, you know—it would be really easy to trip someone and then squash them into that nice hard pavement. I promised I'd do it if she didn't straighten up and stop leaving the pieces for everyone else to pick up."

"And did she?"

"Sweet as pie to the patient. But I'm still going to get her, just on general principle. There's a ten-kilometer race coming up, and I'm going to cream that bitch! She's going to have stitches up her backside from having been run over by a certain unnamed racer who happened to be wearing cleats. And if you tell anyone what I said, I'll say you're lying." Dr. Barnall smiled innocently at Emily, then paused, looking distinctly uncomfortable. Something was apparently bothering him.

"Look, I'm not all that good with social repartee, and I don't have much time to develop it in the middle of this residency. So how about if I just asked you straight out, and then you could tell me to leave you alone?"

"Pardon?" Emily didn't understand in the least what Terry was talking about.

"I'd like to take you out to dinner—or breakfast, as the case may be—and I'd like to do it today. If I wait much longer, I'm going to be finished with the residency and out of this place before I ever have a chance to date you," he said seriously.

"Date me?"

"Yes, you know, like in man-woman, go out together, get to know one another. Remember dating? Like I said, I don't have time for the niceties."

"I'm flattered. Any thirty-year-old woman with a six-year-old daughter would be," Emily said, blushing. She was charmed and a bit surprised. Terry Barnall was nice, warm, friendly, and near her own age. But she hadn't expected him to ask her for a date when there were so many cute, bubbly student nurses around to have fun with.

"How about a nice breakfast at home instead?" she suggested. "I had a meal planned anyway, something with a little body to it, like steak and potatoes. If you're interested, I'd love it if you'd share my meal." She felt excited and awake all of a sudden. Terry was a brilliant, interesting physician, and he was interested in her. This could be fun.

"I'd love to. Let's stop at the store, and I'll pop for some really good steaks. We can hit a deli for some other stuff. Within an hour, you can be fed and ready to throw yourself into bed, and I'll have a good meal under my belt and be ready to come back here for the next grind. Just let me make certain that I can get away. I think Rasin is covering for me, but I'd better check just in case."

Emily nodded, bemused. She watched him as he went over to the house phone to check with Rasin, seeing him in a totally new way, judging him now from the point of view of a woman who was interested in a man rather than a nurse looking at a doctor.

Terry Barnall wasn't anything spectacular to look at, she thought critically. There were plenty of other doctors at Ridge who were more handsome, taller, and better built. Terry was small and wiry. His body reflected his passion for long-distance running. He wasn't exactly handsome, but his thin face was interesting. He could always be counted on to smile and reassure his patients, and his ready humor often calmed everyone during a tense situation. Emily knew better than to make anything out of a chance invitation to a meal, certainly nothing more than friendship, but his straightforward declaration of interest had warmed her. She liked men who didn't play games.

"All set. They've got my pager number, so the hospital can get hold of me if an emergency comes up," Barnall told her. "Come on, let's get the hell out of here before they find something else for me to do—this is the first break I've had in fifty-seven days!" He almost ran toward the exit.

Emily giggled and ran right after him.

They had a grand time shopping for just the right T-bones and looking through the deli for the five kinds of salad they eventually ended up buying. After picking up a big bottle of grape juice, they were ready to go on to Emily's house.

Suddenly Emily was beginning to feel a bit strange about the whole sequence of events. She liked Terry, he was great company, and he liked *her*—he'd said so. But this was the first man she'd even been alone with since her divorce. She had been out of touch with the world of dating for too long to feel completely comfortable. Would he expect to kiss her? What about anything more? Or would they just talk? Emily voted for just talking. Her concern about AIDS had made her decide that she would never make love with a man unless he could prove he was HIV negative to begin with, and then promise to use condoms for the next year, just to be on the safe side. Casual sex was definitely out, even though she had to admit she felt a thrill of interest when she looked at Terry.

"He's probably just out for a good home-cooked meal after fifty-seven days of hospital food," she muttered to herself as she turned the car down the street that led to her house.

"What did you say?"

"Nothing," Emily said quickly. She hadn't meant to say it out loud. That was one of the habits she had gotten into since the divorce—she talked to herself a lot. Most of the one-sided conversation was simply to help her think through her various troubles and to set priorities. She often talked to herself in the car as she was hurrying home, thinking of what had to be done before she left for work the next day. People in other cars sometimes looked at her strangely, but she didn't care. They might think she was crazy, but it kept her sane.

They pulled into the driveway, and Terry whistled.

"Wow! I didn't know I was asking out a rich lady! These houses are expensive." He was honestly awed by the size of her house.

"Yes, it's pretty big. Unfortunately, it's also draining every penny of my savings and then some just to hang onto it until my former husband pays the mortgage off as he was supposed to have done about eight months ago."

"Can't you do something about that? I mean, yell at his attorney or something?"

Emily smiled smugly. "Actually, I can do better than that. Do you know Leopold Peters?"

"Hip-replacement patient? I've seen the name on the board," Terry said.

"Well, he's my husband's attorney, and I spend a lot of time at work planning all the ways I could get revenge on him for the trouble he's given me. He's convinced that I use a harpoon for a syringe! I'm surprised he hasn't hired a taster for his food, and he'll *never* ask me to help him to the bathroom.'' She laughed, remembering how Peters waited until another nurse was in the room before he asked for help, rather than allowing Emily to do anything for him. And every time he was alone with her, he babbled on about how he was going to tell Nicholas Greer to make those alimony payments and get caught up on everything else just as soon as he was out of the hospital. Emily enjoyed every moment of his terror. She knew she should have felt guilty, but she couldn't manage to summon even a drop of pity for the man.

Terry leaned a little closer to her, and put his hand on the back of the car seat. He touched her shoulder, and Emily felt a thrill of anticipation, even though she told herself firmly that there was nothing to anticipate other than a good hot dinner. Then she'd take him back to the hospital and come home and go to sleep.

As Emily began to unlock the door, she heard the phone ringing.

''Damn, I never can get this key to work properly the first time!'' she swore, jiggling the key in the lock and finally making the right connection. ''Bring in the groceries, will you, Terry, while I catch that?'' She ran in the door, hit the light switch, and breathed a sigh of relief. The electric company hadn't gotten around to turning off her power yet. She had sent them the money from the extra day's overtime pay and told them she'd pay the rest at the end of the week. Evidently they'd believed her. Leaving Terry behind, she hurried down the hallway to the kitchen. Just as she grabbed the receiver, the answering machine picked up the call.

"Hang on, please, just let the message run through," Emily said loudly, knowing that she could be heard above the message.

"Mrs. Greer?" the woman on the other end of the line asked.

"Yes. Who is this, please?" Emily said, pointing to the counter where Terry could place the grocery bags.

"Mrs. Greer, this is Ann Forsythe, the school nurse at Dawn Elementary. I was wondering if you could please come in and pick up Colleen. I know she just came back to school a few days ago, but she has a fever, and the cough has come back. I don't want to keep her here where she could spread the infection more than it has been already."

Emily was silent, worrying. Colleen sick again? Her daughter was never sick—what on earth could be going on?

"Mrs. Greer?"

"Yes—of course, I'll be right down," Emily said quickly. So much for her romantic morning interlude.

"Sorry to do this, but I have to go and pick up my little girl," Emily said, turning to Terry. "She just went back to school and now she's come down again with another fever. . . ."

"Think nothing of it. I'll stay here and get the food ready while you pick her up. When you get back, I'll put the steaks on to broil. Besides, I'll enjoy meeting her. I've heard you talk to the other nurses about Colleen. I bet she's just as pretty and nice as her mother."

Emily carried the words with her, cherishing his kindness, all the way to the school. Imagine, she thought, not only did he know she had a daughter and didn't object, he even knew her name! She had purposefully shied away from entanglements since her divorce because she had heard too many stories about men who loved the mothers and hated the kids. She wasn't about to inflict that on her daughter. She'd rather stay single for the rest of her life than cause Colleen a moment's pain.

The nurse was right, Emily decided when she walked into the office. Colleen looked terrible. Her face was flushed, and her eyes were glazed. Even her braids were limp.

"Come on, honey," Emily said, pitying her daughter. Colleen thought that school was the most fun in the world and would never have voluntarily missed a minute of it. "I'll take you to Dr. Peterson, and he'll fix you up." She'd call for an appointment with the pediatrician as soon as she got home. It was time that Colleen was given something to knock out whatever bug she'd had once and for all. Emily knew all the arguments against insisting on medication when the doctor didn't think it was needed, but there were too many times when she thought that, especially with children, doctors erred too much on the side of conservative medicine.

Emily carried Colleen up the front stairs, and was met at the door by Terry, who took the child from her. He felt the fever and looked at her over Colleen's head, his eyes reflecting the concern that Emily herself felt.

"How about a nice cool bath and then straight into bed?" he suggested. "If the fever doesn't come down, then it's time for the pediatrician."

Emily immediately called for an appointment anyway.

"Mrs. Greer, the only thing I can tell you to do is bring Colleen in, and we'll fit you in when you get here. Doctor has been so backed up that I won't even pretend that we have open time on the books. It's hit or miss, and frankly, I hope about fifteen kids this morning miss their appointments. It would take that much for us to catch up. And to top it all off, the doctor has to leave at three this afternoon for a medical convention in New York," the nurse told her.

Soon afterward, Emily had bathed Colleen and settled her on the couch to watch television, wrapped in a blanket and sipping ginger ale. Colleen's temperature had dropped from 103 to 100, but Emily knew it could shoot back up within a matter of minutes. Still, the little girl seemed to be feeling much better, and Emily was actually able to enjoy her meal with Terry Barnall, joking and laughing as if they were old buddies.

Terry, she noticed approvingly, was very much at home in the kitchen. True to his word, he grilled the steaks just the way Emily liked them—charred on the outside and rare in the middle. He'd even found place mats, silverware, plates, and glasses, so Emily had nothing to do but relax and eat. She couldn't help contrasting that with Nicholas, who had never set foot in the kitchen. Cooking, according to Nicholas Greer, was women's work.

"I really appreciate this, Terry," she said now. "The steak is absolutely delicious."

Terry grinned. "I'm not exactly what you'd call a gourmet chef, but there's no way I'm going to ruin a nice, juicy steak. I don't cook much for myself, though—no time. When I'm not on duty, I'm either running or sleeping. At the moment, sleeping is at the top of my list of priorities. I'm really beat, especially after this last marathon."

"The fifty-seven days?"

"That's the one. I know it's supposed to be only a

thirty-six-hour shift and then time off, but it's been so hectic this week that all of us have just worked flat out until we dropped. We'd take a little time off, then the beeper would sound, and there we were again, practically sleeping on our feet during surgery."

As if it had been jogged into awareness, his beeper went off, cutting through the conversation.

Terry sighed, getting to his feet.

From what she could hear of the mumbled conversation, it didn't sound good. Apparently there had been a multiple-car accident, and severe head traumas and other neurosurgical disasters were waiting for him at the hospital.

"Emily . . ." Terry shook his head apologetically when he hung up the phone.

"Not another word. I know how it is with you guys. Here—take some of this potato salad with you and stick it in the refrigerator for when you're out of the operating room." Emily put the lid back on the container and handed it to him, then called into the living room, "Colleen, come on, honey. I'm taking you to Dr. Peterson after we drop Dr. Barnall off at the hospital."

And then, she said silently, she'd finally come home and go to bed. Alone.

Chapter Eight

"Coralie, please, you have to tell us what happened. Think how bad we'd feel if your injury was caused by a nurse. What if there was a nurse who wasn't taking proper care of his or her patients—we can't let that happen, can we?" Keith tried again to break through the old woman's reserve, but Coralie turned her face away and stared out at the blackness beyond the hospital window.

"It wasn't a nurse. I keep telling you people, it wasn't anything a nurse or a doctor did. Why can't you just put it down to the fact that my old bones break easily?" She sounded weary, and for the first time, there wasn't any bounce in her voice. Even her face looked as if she had aged ten years in the past day. She had put aside her gardening books and seed catalogues, and Keith had found the order forms discarded in the trash sack.

"Please?" Keith asked again.

"No."

He sighed and finished changing the IV tubing. He'd taken an extra long time with the task in order to attempt to pry some more information out of Coralie. But she still wouldn't talk, and that in itself made Keith suspicious. Coralie Cooper had always been like an open book, ready and eager to share everything with the people around her. He couldn't shake the feeling that it was something far more serious than a break that had happened at an awkward time. It wasn't just brittle bones. Something else was wrong, and he had to find out what.

He straightened the bed clothes for her and reached over to plump the extra pillow that she rested her hand on when the IV hurt.

Keith frowned and looked at the pillow more closely. Something had crackled when he hit it with his hand to bring it back into shape. Something long and rectangular seemed to be tucked inside the case. He patted the pillow again, and then began to reach inside the cotton case to make certain there wasn't anything in there that could hurt her. Strange things had been known to end up pressed inside the pillow cases when the laundry got just a little lax with their supervision.

Coralie yelped and grabbed the pillow away from him, holding it against her thin chest.

"It's fine. Don't bother, I'll take care of this." Coralie tried to conceal her alarm as she pushed it under her arm so he couldn't touch it. With the pillow protected, she lay back against the raised head of the bed and closed her eyes.

"I'm so tired, Keith," she sighed. "I've never been so tired in my life. What do you think they're putting in that pain-killer you're giving me?"

Keith just shrugged. He knew that it wasn't any

medication that made Coralie tired. It was the fact that, whatever had happened, it had taken the spirit out of Coralie. Suddenly she was a querulous old woman—an old woman with a secret, Keith thought as he looked at the pillow.

He filed the incident away to be thought about when he had the time. What could she possibly be so desperate to hide from him?

The first part of Keith's shift was the usual run of medications, checking the piggy backs for extra medications to be infused through the IV lines, taking vital signs, and giving an occasional back rub. Keith's back rubs were in great demand during the night shift—patients who couldn't get to sleep even with pills could drift off in a matter of minutes under his skilled hands. Keith had developed his massage technique when he was a wrestler. More than once he or his partners had been thrown, stomped, bruised, and battered beyond their wildest expectations. Having someone around who could ease the pain and coax the contracted muscles into movement again was essential, so Keith and one other partner in the tag team had learned the skill of massage. He had never expected it to translate into something that could help patients.

It was just about time for a well-deserved rest when Keith heard the soft chime of the patient call button. He looked up and saw that the light above the room shared by Cynda Arden and Lara Mendoza was lit. Lara Mendoza hadn't required much care in the past few days. The doctor was keeping her in the hospital to test some new drugs on her. Some of the medications had left her groggy, and she preferred to be left alone, anyway. Keith was glad to grant her every bit of privacy that she asked for.

Lara wasn't the most communicative patient Keith had ever had. She would answer a direct question, but never volunteered any information. Most patients were delighted to talk about their family, their pets, their lives outside of the hospital, but not Lara. She seemed to exist in a little world all her own, where everything revolved around her own wants and desires. She seemed to have no need to share any of that world with anyone else. She even resented sharing a room with another patient.

Keith shrugged. It wasn't his problem. He didn't have to live with her. Her husband seemed to be perfectly happy with the way Lara behaved, encouraging her belief that the world centered on her. The woman had more fancy nightgowns, more flowers, and more books than any patient that Keith had ever seen. He could tell from the way that her husband responded to her every demand that Lara Mendoza had, for some reason, developed into a professional patient.

"Thank God she's not *my* wife," Keith said under his breath. He could put up with it because he could leave it all behind when he went home. Besides, patients had every right to be left in privacy, as long as their need for solitude didn't interfere with giving the medications that the doctor ordered.

Keith hurried into the room, looking automatically over at Lara. She was sound asleep.

"Knew the light had to be you, Cynda—you're the only one who would be up at this hour of the morning," Keith said lightly. He liked Cynda Arden. She was the exact opposite of Lara, dynamic and interested in everything and everyone around her. She had been a patient on the floor several times before, and Keith enjoyed her company. He never allowed himself to dwell on the fact that, as a cystic-fibrosis patient, her life could be abruptly ended at any time.

Cynda was sitting up in bed, her legs bent into the basic yoga sitting position. She finished two stitches, and back-stitched twice before cutting the thread on the quilt she was working on. The colors of the design were like Cynda herself when she was feeling good—bright and warm and appealing.

Right now, though, Keith noticed Cynda's face was pale and drawn. She was only twenty-two, but he could already see the ravages of cystic fibrosis. She was painfully thin, and her complexion had a gray tinge. Her hair, however, was still shining bright and blond, and she had fastened it with pretty rainbow barrettes to keep it out of her eyes.

Keith walked over to the bed and flipped off the call light. "What do you need, Cynda? It's not time for medication, and you just ate, so it has to be something else."

"Brilliant deduction, Watson!" Cynda smiled wanly at him. "I need to be pounded. I know it was done just about three hours ago, but it's definitely necessary." She stopped to catch her breath. "Things are closing in again." She folded up her needlework and laid it carefully aside on the long, narrow table beside the bed. The table was covered with a neat stack of textbooks, a television guide, a sewing kit, and several other personal belongings. The organization of the table was the mark of someone who had been in the hospital many times and had learned to make the best of the limited space afforded by one bed, one table, and one small chest that was usually filled with medical supplies.

Cynda grabbed a pillow and leaned forward so Keith could start the treatment that would drain her lungs of the heavy mucus that had been building up more and more often in the past few days. She had been through the pounding and coughing and pills and aerosols for years. By now she knew the whole routine so well that she could have done it herself if she could have reached her own back.

The percussion of the lungs began with Keith's cupped hands beating against her shoulders and upper back. As she began to cough, she moved into other positions that would allow all ten sections of the lungs to be cleansed so she could breathe easily and perhaps last through the night without another treatment.

"Damn, I hate having to work around an IV," Cynda complained mildly as she lay on her stomach, with her whole body tilting downward. "I know I need antibiotics for the pneumonia again, but wouldn't you think by now the bugs would stay away from me? I'm sure I'm just one big walking bread mold." She stopped to cough.

"Will you guys shut up over there? That's positively disgusting!" Lara Mendoza was sitting up in bed and glaring over at Cynda. It was obvious that she disliked the younger woman. Lara's face was a mask of disdain. With her black hair pulled back in a neat bun and dressed in a deep red caftan that she wore in lieu of a nightgown, she might have stepped right out of a painting of a Spanish noblewoman.

Same arrogance as the nobility, too—no one else mattered but her, Keith thought. He wanted to point out to Lara that she had needed care once or twice, too, during her stay in the hospital, and no one had made snotty comments about *her*. Why should she make Cynda feel uncomfortable? But nurses weren't allowed to say anything. They were supposed to listen and nod and be pleasant, no matter what the provocation from a patient. The only time he could intervene was if Cynda asked him to intervene. And Cynda would never do that.

Cynda looked over at the other bed and gestured with her palms up, signaling mutely that she couldn't do anything about her need for treatment at this hour of the night.

"Sorry," Cynda wheezed when she could speak and grabbed the aerosol inhaler. "I'm not too fond of the sounds myself."

But Lara was obviously spoiling for a fight. She didn't want Cynda to accept her comments with equanimity.

"I don't care about what *you* think about the sounds, *I* think they're revolting! I don't see why they don't put you in a private room, so it doesn't bother anyone else when you have to have your treatment." She paused for a second to see if she had produced the desired effect. As far as Lara could tell, there was no reason why she should be subjected to this horrible coughing and clearing out of the lungs. There was a special ward for people like Cynda, and Lara couldn't for the life of her understand why Cynda hadn't been put there with others of her own kind. However, since that was not the case, Lara was determined to see that her roommate knew Lara Mendoza was in charge. She continued, "And I'd appreciate it if you turned off that light. I can't sleep with a light shining in my eyes."

Keith, who had his back to Lara, rolled his eyes heavenward. He knew she was ill, but did she have to be just plain mean, too?

Cynda looked over at Lara and shrugged in apology.

"I'll draw the curtains, then. But I have finals

coming up in school, and I'm not going to blow the last half of my senior year just because you don't like the light," Cynda said, her voice cool.

Lara humphed. "I can't understand why they let you go to college, if you've got a disease that's so serious. *I* never went to college and I didn't miss it."

Cynda stared at the woman in disbelief. This was definitely not going to be one of her better hospital visits, she could tell. She could have gone to the CF ward, but she had wanted to stay away from it for a while. Sometimes she made a specific request to be with other CF kids, but right now she needed a break from the atmosphere of the Cystic Fibrosis Section of the hospital. The nurses in the special ward were great—they tried to make it a happy place. But the last time Cynda had been there, one of the girls she had known since they were both thirteen had died. Her body had finally given up the fight, as it did in so many kids before they reached their twenties. Cynda had decided she couldn't face another stay in the ward just yet.

Keith saw the play of emotions on Cynda's face and wished he could break just once the unwritten rule that nurses were not to interfere in patient relations. He'd like to tell Lara Mendoza what he thought of her and her acid tongue.

He'd better not. But he could attempt to distract Cynda from the woman's comments.

"What are you making? A quilt?" Keith glanced down at the fine handwork Cynda had folded and placed on the table.

"It's for my niece—or nephew. We're not certain which yet. My sister and her husband are adopting. In fact, there's a rumor that it could be twins, and if it is, I don't know what I'm going to do. All this work twice over?" Cynda spread the quilt out on the bed. It was a pretty pattern of yellow, blue, and pink blocks arranged so that it looked as if the blocks were tumbling right down the middle of the quilt.

"That should drive the kid crazy as soon as he or she can focus on the design. Good training for a future mathematician, did you know that?" Keith touched the design.

"What do you mean?"

"There was a study in a medical journal I read recently that said children who are stimulated early and often with geometric shapes and puzzles perform better on IQ tests later in life. So you're starting the baby out right."

"I hope so. I've done enough to mess things up for my sister and her husband—" Cynda stopped short.

Keith heard the sadness in her voice.

"Want to tell me about it?" he asked gently.

Cynda shrugged and looked down at the quilt.

"Nothing much to tell. You know I've got CF, and you probably also know it's a genetically linked disease. We've been told that the doctors can't tell who's carrying that gene and who's going to have CF kids, until it's too late to do anything about it."

"And?" Keith prodded.

Cynda traced the design of the quilt, her fingers moving over the shapes as if somehow they had the answer to the problem. "My sister decided not to have children of her own. She and her husband have to adopt because their kids could turn out like me. And, Keith, I wouldn't want this for anyone in the world!" Cynda whispered. She would have cried, but she tried never to allow herself to get to the teary stage, or she might not stop for days on end. And who needed a weepy patient, anyway?

"There's nothing wrong with you," Keith tried to reassure her.

"There may not be anything wrong with the me that's in my brain, but this old body has plenty wrong with it! I've read all the books. I don't have a hell of a lot of chance to live through the next ten years, much less any longer than that. My body doesn't digest anything too well, and I keep having pneumonia. Does that sound like I'm a good long-term risk?"

"Yes," Keith said firmly. "I've watched a couple of CF kids come through here who beat the odds, and you're just the type to do it. Look at you—you're going to school, you're active, you have hobbies. I'll even bet you have pets just waiting to snuggle up with you when you get out of here."

"Yes . . . three cats," Cynda said, thinking of her two Siamese and one Abyssinian who were waiting for her at home. If she knew them, they were probably curled up on her bed right now. She hoped her mother had remembered to turn on the electric blanket—they all liked the heat.

Keith smiled. "Well, that's just the kind of patient profile we like to see. So don't you dare let the early-morning horribles get you down, girl. You just take a few more stitches on that quilt, and then lie back and relax and get to sleep. You'll make it."

Keith turned to go. As he pulled back the curtain, he looked over at Lara, expecting to see her glaring at him. Instead, Lara's right hand was shaking and her face was set in a grimace as she began to have a seizure. He immediately rang the button for help and rolled her over onto her side. Gently he restrained her right arm, which was beating against the padded rails of the bed.

"Is everything all right?" Cynda parted the curtains and peered out as Keith grabbed the tongue board from the top of the bed while he tried to keep Lara from turning herself onto her back.

Denise Frazier raced into the room, answering the call.

"What do you need?" she asked briskly.

"I think we're all right. I hit the button out of instinct. Actually, this isn't nearly as bad as a couple she's had," Keith said.

"Look, if you can handle it alone, please do, because there are about eight Gypsies out in the hall demanding to see their uncle. I haven't a clue who they're talking about. Anyway, they need help," Denise said and dashed out of the room.

Keith could see why Denise never had a problem with her weight—the calories never had a chance to settle down and rest.

He could feel the change in Lara's seizure as he held her arm, establishing contact to assess her physically. He pumped the blood-pressure cuff once again, watching for any signs of either unusually high or low pressure.

Gradually the flailing of the hand stopped, and the leg tremors that accompanied the seizure subsided. He listened critically to Lara's respiration. At the first signs of screeching or whistling in the throat, or any other sign of distress, he would have called for more backup. But he heard nothing more than the normal, slightly deepened panting that accompanied most epileptic seizures. After all, it was a physical strain and the body reacted to that strain by needing more oxygen.

The tremors finally stopped altogether, and Lara closed her eyes, her face slack and somehow younger looking. She rubbed at her arm where she had repeatedly hit the padded rail. There would be a big bruise there tomorrow, she knew, but she'd cover it up with one of her long-sleeved gowns. Then no one would know she had hurt herself. It had been a remarkably short seizure, though. From start to finish, as far as Lara could tell, it had lasted only about forty-five seconds.

It was ironic, she thought, that she could control everything else—her husband, her servants, her life —but she couldn't control her own body.

Lara opened her eyes and waved Keith away from the bed. "I'm okay now. It was a small one this time, just a couple of jiggles, really. The medications are working," she said.

"How long do you think it took?" Keith asked, though he had timed the seizure from the moment he became aware of the movement of her hand.

"About a minute, maybe less than that."

Keith noted her guess on the pad. It was considered a good sign when the patient was aware of the duration, and Lara had timed it almost exactly.

"No trouble with orientation. I know where I am and what day it is," she said, providing him with the hospital's name and the date.

"Any aura? Any kind of warning that the seizure was about to start?"

"A little one—not nearly the kind that I've been having. This time it was just a gradual lessening of the light, not the tunnel vision I've had a couple of times. The sharp odor wasn't so bad, either. In fact, I don't think I even noticed it this time," Lara answered. "And there's another difference. Normally I wouldn't be able to talk after one of these things. I just go to sleep. But this time I'm awake, at least for now."

Keith noted all the changes in the chart. He'd give the information to the nurse on the next shift. The doctor would be glad to know that at least one of the medications he'd prescribed seemed to be controlling the seizures.

He wondered why Lara didn't seem pleased when

she talked about the improvement the new medication had made. It couldn't be that she actually enjoyed being the poor, pitiful patient all the time, could it? Wouldn't a grown woman eventually get tired of telling everyone about every single sniffle, tic, and wheeze she experienced from the time she got up in the morning until she went to bed at night? Wouldn't she want to get on with her life and do something other than eat, breathe, and think about her sickness?

Keith had seen "professional patients" before, but few carried it to such extremes. He had stayed late one morning, and had overheard Lara talking with her doctor about her headaches. They seemed to be transient, and caused no damage that would show up on any kind of test. She described them very precisely and at great length as the doctor listened politely, but Keith had seen the doctor's face and knew he had tuned Lara out.

Later, without naming names, he had discussed Lara with one of his friends. "That woman hasn't got a clue that the rest of the world feels those kinds of aches and pains all the time, too. She's certain no one else could possibly feel the way she does and still manage to function."

"And you think that isn't normal? Look at all the upwardly mobiles who decide the only way they can stand their little tics and pains is to take drugs. But it's usually because they're convinced that they can't really cope, and that no one else has problems like theirs. Sad, isn't it?"

"But damn it, she's making herself into an invalid for no reason at all. Not even the best of influences will ever change her, because she's got her husband so brainwashed into seeing her as a poor, sick baby that she'll never be anything else."

Keith stayed with Lara for a while longer to make certain she wasn't going to slip into another seizure. He left only to pour out the meds that were due. Finally, however, he was confident that it was safe to leave.

Cynda waited until he had gone, then pulled back the curtain.

Lara quickly turned over so that her back was to the girl.

"That was quite a way to start the night, wasn't it?" Cynda said.

"I don't want to talk about it," Lara answered frostily.

"No, you probably don't. But would you mind telling me something? I've got a disease that makes me cough up a lot of gunk from my chest and I make disgusting sounds that even my best friends hate. But I live with it. *You* have a disease that makes you unable to control your movements for a while and make disgusting noises, and then it passes, leaving you tired and unhappy about the whole mess. Now, would you mind telling me what makes *you* such a damned fine human being, and *me* the scum of the earth, just because our diseases have different names?"

"I didn't say that."

"You didn't have to say it in so many words. The bitching you do when I have my treatments are enough of a clue to how you feel."

Lara still refused to turn over. She didn't want to look at Cynda—she knew from the way the nurses acted that they liked Cynda better than they did her. Cynda never caused trouble and harsh words usually never left her mouth.

But Lara finally answered Cynda's question. "I

don't really think you're bad. And it isn't your disease that bothers me. I guess it's your attitude."

Cynda was so astonished she couldn't even laugh. This bitter, manipulative woman was telling *her* she had the wrong attitude?

"Would you care to explain?" she said at last.

Now Lara turned over and looked at Cynda, her eyes hard as onyx. She was going to enjoy telling Cynda just what she thought of the girl's sickly-sweet Pollyanna outlook.

"You're not being realistic with yourself about your life. When I look at you, I see a girl who's riding for the same kind of fall I took when I was your age. You think the world is going to welcome you with open arms and tell you how wonderful and brave you are. But it isn't going to happen that way. It's stupid to think things can be different for people like you and me!"

"What are you talking about?" Cynda was genuinely bewildered.

"I'm talking about this college stuff that you're doing, and the quilts and all that. Why are you pushing yourself? It won't do any good. There's nobody out there in the business world, in the *real* world, who will accept you as a normal person." Lara shook her head when Cynda tried to interrupt, "No, listen to me. You're a *sick* person and that's all they have to know about you. You'll never be able to get a job. You'll never have a career. Why kid yourself?"

Cynda said quietly, "I don't do it to *prove* anything to the rest of the world. I do it for *me*." How could she possibly explain the fierce need she felt to make something worthwhile of the time she had left?

Even when Cynda was a child spending time in CF wards, she had watched the other kids in the ward.

She had soon realized that the patients who were involved and interested in various projects might not have healed faster than the other kids, but their stay in the hospital was more fun than it was for the kids who just lay in bed, waiting to have something happen to them.

Lara wasn't interested in Cynda's brief explanation. "What's the reason for trying? You aren't going to gain anything. You're not going to accomplish anything. The world isn't going to change for little Cynda Arden, the brave but fragile heroine in her own soap opera. It sure as hell didn't change for *me!*"

Cynda shrugged. "Maybe what you want out of life is different from what I want. I don't have any desire to be a soap-opera character. I just want to know that when I take those last few breaths that are going to hurt and leave me choking and then finally dying, I've done everything that I could with the life I was given." Surely Lara could understand that. Hadn't she ever thought about death? Cynda had decided long ago that since she was going to die young, she was going to leave some kind of mark on the world, even if it was only a crib quilt for an unknown baby and a set of straight-A grades in the hardest classes her college had to offer.

Lara didn't even dignify Cynda's words with an answer.

Now Cynda was beginning to get mad. Most of the time she ignored people like Lara, but this woman was truly infuriating. "What are you going to be able to say *you've* done with your life?" she asked.

"I've done all right so far," Lara said coolly.

"Sure, you have," Cynda said. "You've found a husband who's willing to wait on you hand and foot. You've removed all challenges from your life. I heard you say once that your husband can't really afford it, but you have a housemaid and a cook and someone to drive you around if you decide you want to go out. Are you proud of that?"

Lara was instantly defensive. "It's what he wants to do for me. He's said so a hundred times. He wants to make me comfortable."

"What's so wonderful about being coddled and comfortable all the time?"

"It beats hurting!"

"Not if it means there's no challenge. Tell me, Lara—when you finally lie there in bed, dying, what are you going to be able to look back on and say, 'Against all odds, I accomplished *this*.' What are you going to point to with pride and say, 'I did it! I pushed myself and I learned and I fought and I won!' " Cynda paused to catch her breath. She knew she was overexerting, but she didn't care. "Nothing, that's what you'll have to be proud of. Nothing at all."

She grabbed the curtain and pulled it around her bed, leaving Lara to stare at the cloth barrier.

Chapter Nine

"Time to check your IV, Mr. Peters," Emily said as she hurried into Leopold Peters's room. She was concerned about Coralie Cooper and wanted to finish up with everyone else so she could spend a little time with the old woman. Keith hadn't been able to find out what was wrong and had asked Emily for help. But worrying about Coralie wasn't going to stop Emily from having her nightly fun at Peters' expense. She fixed him with a glare. "I'd just like you to know that every day since you were assigned to me, I've gone home and looked in the mail, anticipating a nice big fat check from my ex-husband. It hasn't been there." Emily wagged her finger at him. "I thought you were going to tell him to pay what he owes me?"

Peters shrank back against the mattress, and his features began to fade toward gray.

To Emily it was a game, harmless because she knew she was giving him the best care she could in spite of how she felt about him personally. But Emily wasn't certain *he* knew that she was playing. She unfailingly told him about not hearing from Nicholas, and then managed to find some painful procedure that needed to be done, if possible. Peters had survived her injections and establishing a new IV. He had even allowed her to walk with him to the bathroom. But every second she was in the room, he looked terrified of what might be coming next. And all because he had a guilty conscience.

Serves him right, she thought smugly.

"The IV is fine—don't worry about it." Peters was beginning to sweat. He tried to hide his arm from her, but the unwieldy board that kept his elbow straight got in the way and twisted his arm into an uncomfortable angle.

"Just have to check it out," Emily said as she traced the lines that led from the bag down through the IV monitoring machine and into the vein.

Peters tried to move away from her, an impossible task in a bed that was barely wide enough for him to begin with, and winced as a spasm of pain cut through him.

"Damn, that hurt!" he muttered. He hadn't been prepared for the knifelike anguish that suddenly ripped through his hip joint.

"Having a little trouble? There are still orders for an *injection* of pain meds, if that's what you want," Emily offered helpfully, stressing the word "injection."

Peters failed to rise to the bait. He had blanched even more under his ruddy tan, and looked both startled and pained, as if he couldn't believe what was happening to him. He pushed at his groin area and then looked up at Emily again. He was sweating profusely now, even though the room was cool, and his lips were pinched and white.

"I think something happened . . . " he finally managed to say.

Emily stared at the man intently. Up until this moment, she'd been joking with him, even if he didn't know it. But from the lines around his mouth and the pallor of his skin, this was no joke. Something was definitely wrong.

Suddenly she was all business. "Please describe your pain."

Peters wet his lips, wishing that the nurse was anyone at all other than Emily. She'd probably enjoy watching him writhe in agony, and right now it was all he could do to keep from screaming. It felt as if a knife had decided to take up permanent residence in the hip socket.

"It's my hip. I moved sideways and I felt something crunch. . . ." Peters licked his lips again. He wished he hadn't eaten dinner. Every bite he had taken seemed to be about to come back up. It was the pain—he was dizzy with it. It washed over him, radiating from the site of the replacement.

Emily pulled back the blanket and checked as well as she could for any kind of visible change. She attempted to get a pulse and found one easily, but that didn't mean that something hadn't happened at the site of the operation, underneath the skin where she couldn't possibly check.

"Mr. Peters, I'm going to place a call to Dr. Mendelsohn for instructions. Until then, please do not attempt to move. Where there is pain, there's always a chance of damage. I'm certain the doctor will be right in to see what's going on."

Emily left the room, and Peters relaxed. Gradually

his hands unclenched as the discomfort eased fractionally. Emily Greer had actually listened to him. She knew he was in trouble and instead of allowing him to linger in agony, she had gone to call the doctor. Maybe, his pain-fogged mind concluded, just maybe he had been wrong in his treatment of her in the courtroom. . . .

Dr. Mendelsohn was at the hospital within fifteen minutes. He was, as always, perfectly groomed, in a suit, white shirt, tie, and shined shoes. No matter what time of day or night he came in, Mendelsohn was always impeccably groomed. It had become his trademark, and occasionally there would be informal bets made among the nurses during the dead of night, if he would come in wearing a shirt, tie, and suit, if they called at three in the morning.

Emily checked the clock. Only *two* in the morning, but she could use it when she bet that he would always come in perfectly dressed. His fastidiousness carried over into his care of his patients, too. He was thoughtful, careful, and knew every new procedure and treatment in the area of orthopedics.

"If you would come with me, please?" He motioned to Emily, and hurried into the room.

"So, what have you done, Mr. Peters?" He ran his hand over the man's toes, feeling for the temperature of the skin and Mr. Peters's responsiveness to stimuli.

"I moved sideways. Shouldn't have done a thing to me. I've been moving around for a couple of days now—but this time I couldn't believe the pain." The lawyer's voice was almost back to its booming courtroom timbre, and his pallor had subsided a bit.

"Have you moved since it happened?" the doctor asked.

"No."

"Well, try just a gentle movement, maybe just

swinging your pelvis slightly to the left,'' Mendelsohn suggested.

Peters tried the movement and bit back a scream. His hands were gripping the sheets so hard he was actually almost ripping them. "I can't . . . I can't move, it hurts too much. It's worse than when I came in originally!" he moaned.

Dr. Mendelsohn sighed. "Emily, please call X ray and tell them we have an emergency. I think the first pictures should be taken while Mr. Peters is still in this bed. And then if it shows what I think it will, we'll be down to surgery.''

Peters was watching them in near panic. "What is it? What's happened?''

"Nothing we could have anticipated. There are some cases, very few cases, that simply don't work the first time through the mill. Remember the ball and socket I showed you when you came into my office for your first appointment?''

Peters nodded.

"I believe the ball has slipped out of the socket. It sometimes happens, though very rarely. Occasionally the muscles just cannot hold everything in place— perhaps the socket isn't ground down quite far enough, or the placement isn't perfect—there are a lot of reasons. But the end result is that you think you're just about to get back on your feet, and wham, it's out again. So we go in and repair it, and the second time around, everything works fine.''

"It should have been fine the *first* time around!" Peters growled. "I don't want to have to go through all this again. Why the hell can't things be done right the first time, instead of making a patient go back in for more surgery? It's damned bad medicine, that's what it is!''

Dr. Mendelsohn shrugged. "It's not bad medicine,

it's just something unforeseen that occasionally happens. I'm not any happier about this than you are—
I'd like all my surgeries to be perfect every time."

"I should have been told about this possibility! Why didn't you tell me it might fail and I'd end up back on the cutting board, laid out for you to fillet my bones again?"

"Mr. Peters, I'm certain that you read the informed consent paper we gave you, outlining the risks of surgery?" Mendelsohn was no longer smiling.

"Sure, I did. But I also know that if someone does a bad job, that informed risk consent isn't worth the paper it's written on. Tell me, Mendelsohn, have you ever been sued for malpractice?" Peters glared at the doctor.

Dr. Mendelsohn stood up slowly. He stared down at the attorney, and took several deep breaths before he was able to answer.

"Mr. Peters, that is none of your business. However, since you seem to be unhappy with the work I have done on your hip, I suggest you call in another surgeon to take over the case from now on, because I'm not going to touch you again."

Peters looked stunned. It had never occurred to him that he could end up without a doctor. He had chosen Dr. Mendelsohn specifically because, in all the inquiries he had made, he had repeatedly been told that this man was the best orthopedic surgeon around. He'd been throwing his weight around, trying to scare the doctor into working a little harder this time, but he didn't want Mendelsohn off the case.

"You can't just walk away from me and leave me here in pain. You wouldn't do that, you're supposed to be the best in the business . . . " he blustered.

"Oh yes, I can walk away from you. No doctor is

136

obligated to work with a patient who does not trust his skill in handling a case, and who is threatened with legal action if the case does not proceed smoothly. There are no guarantees in medicine. That's why it's called the *practice* of medicine—we're still learning and practicing until the day we retire. And as for me being the best, you're going to have to take second best, or third best, or maybe even whoever they have on staff over at County Hospital if I can't find someone here tonight. Because, Mr. Peters, I'm not on the case any longer, as of right now."

Dr. Mendelsohn motioned for Emily to follow him out of the room. He marched down the hallway without looking either right or left.

"Emily, will you please place calls to several of the other bone men on the staff? I recommend Cather or Willis. Use your discretion, but get someone, because I'm not going to talk to that son of a bitch again."

Emily stared at Dr. Mendelsohn, flabbergasted. She hadn't thought the gentle, kind doctor even *knew* swear words. Nothing had ever rattled him before, not even the most grievous of accidents or the worst of complications. She was terribly angry at Peters for lashing out at this doctor, of all men. Dr. Mendelsohn didn't deserve that kind of treatment.

She looked at Dr. Mendelsohn's furious face, and smiled—not at his anger, but at the thought of Peters having made such a terrible mistake. He had finally done it to himself! He had opened his mouth and let the words stream out without thinking about their possible effect—and here he was, in pain and without a doctor.

"Get the men on the line, and if they accept the case, I'll fill them in on the details. I won't talk to them until then. I don't want any prejudice against the bastard, because he needs help now with that hip. As for the X ray, wait on that and medications and anything else until he has a different physician." Dr. Mendelsohn paused, and then, though it was obvious he didn't want to say it, he added, "Of course, if you can't find another surgeon, I'll be forced to come back in and do something for the man, at least make him comfortable. I can't walk away from a patient who is in trouble."

Emily nodded, and decided to risk asking for medications. "He does seem to be in pain right now . . . " she said timidly.

"I don't care if he's *dying* right now, I'm not going to prescribe so much as an aspirin! Try and find another physician first. Or maybe Mr. Peters would like to call around and try and get his own doctor. Maybe he'd even like to leave. As a matter of fact, I'd be delighted if he hauled himself out of that bed and walked out of here and out of Ridge. Imagine that man saying such a thing! Malpractice!" Dr. Mendelsohn's face was dull red and his blue eyes were steely with rage.

"Yes, sir," Emily said and turned to the telephone. She knew she'd find another bone man to take over, but until then, Peters could damn well stew in his own juice. He'd lit the fire himself!

But ten minutes later, she still hadn't managed to find an orthopedic surgeon who was willing to take the case. When they asked who the initial physician had been and learned that it was Mendelsohn, the best hip-replacement man in the Midwest, they bowed out one by one. Doctors have an instinct about some cases, and this one smelled to high heaven. If Mendelsohn wouldn't handle it, it was either too dangerous or too complicated for them even to think about.

Dr. Mendelsohn had left the desk, but finally came back to find out Emily's progress.

"I'm sorry—no one wants him. They all ask for a little information, and then they say they would rather not accept the case. No one will turn it down if it is an emergency, if requested, but they don't want him as a regular patient."

Mendelsohn muttered an expletive. "Okay, get Cather on the line again. I'll talk to him. He'll take it as a personal favor. But if Peters opens his mouth to Cather about malpractice, he's likely to end up being sent over to County, instead of staying here at Ridge."

Emily left Dr. Mendelsohn to call Cather and work out the details while she went back in to check on her patient.

"What's he doing? Is he going to take me down to surgery? Where are the X-ray people?" Peters demanded, all bluster.

"Mr. Peters, I have just spent fifteen minutes on the phone trying to find a physician who will take your case. It's only because Dr. Mendelsohn intervened himself that we found one who would accept you as a patient at this hospital. If he hadn't stepped in, you'd have been shipped off to County, where they have to treat you."

"I could force you to keep me here!"

"Yes, but you couldn't force the doctors to take your case."

Peters was outraged. "Being treated this way is against the Hippocratic Oath. Doctors have to take care of the sick and injured. . . ."

"Not if the sick and injured threaten them, and you did that in front of a witness, Mr. Peters!"

Peters was beginning to get the feeling that for the first time in his life he had been beaten, and most of it was his own fault. He didn't take gracefully to being the one who had caused these problems in the first place—he was used to bullying his way through the world.

"And you'd definitely testify against me, wouldn't you?"

Emily laughed. "After what you did to me in the divorce case, you'd even ask such a question? You lied, you cheated, you've even advised my husband not to pay what he owes me, and you have to ask what I'd say if there was a deposition taken on what happened tonight?"

"No, I guess I don't need to ask."

Peters tried to move and bit back a scream.

"Can I get a shot, at least? That doctor wouldn't leave me in pain, would he?"

"No shot until Dr. Cather comes in and orders it. Sorry," Emily said.

"This is outrageous! You can't deny me medication when I hurt! I'll sue you, too!"

"I believe those were the very words that started this whole thing originally," Emily said tartly.

"Get Dr. Mendelsohn back in here! He can't abandon me like this. He's responsible! Wait until the hospital administration hears about this," Peters said. His voice, however, had begun to lose a little of its stridency.

"Mr. Peters, I'll say this to you only once, and only because you seem to have trouble comprehending why your actions are so detrimental to your care," Emily said, lowering her voice. "You have insulted a man who is perhaps one of the best physicians this hospital has ever had on staff. You've threatened him with a malpractice lawsuit for no reason at all, and you have questioned his actions in relation to you as a patient. Once you did that, Dr. Mendelsohn had no choice except to walk off the case. He cannot treat a patient who threatens him and questions his competency. Getting a second opinion is one thing, but once you have committed yourself to his care, you don't attempt to intimidate the man."

"But it was a joke," Peters protested weakly.

"It isn't a joke to a physician. As a result of your 'joke,' which caused Dr. Mendelsohn to remove himself from the case, we have only one other staff physician, Dr. Cather, who might possibly, as a personal favor to Dr. Mendelsohn, accept the case on an emergency basis. When I called the other doctors, they all questioned me about Dr. Mendelsohn's reasons for leaving the case. I told them there was a concern about treatment, nothing else. When they heard that, they were unwilling to consider it since if you doubt the treatment given you by Dr. Mendelsohn, you would obviously not be happy with treatment from anyone else."

Peters lay back in the bed and closed his eyes.

"I'll wait for Cather."

"Good idea," Emily said dryly.

Chapter Ten

"Emily, there's a call for you from Emergency," Denise called to her from the desk as Emily left Peters's room.

"Emergency? I'll be right there."

She picked up the phone. "This is Emily Greer. You have a call for me?"

"Yes, Mrs. Greer, one moment please." The nurse on the other end put her on hold for a few seconds, and then someone else came on the line.

"Emily, is that you?"

"*Nora*? What's going on?" Emily felt a tightening sensation in her chest. Had something happened to Colleen? But the little girl had been sleeping soundly when Emily had left for work. Colleen had still been running a slight temperature, but the pediatrician had assured Emily it was nothing more than a touch of the flu.

"I think you'd better come down here, Emily. Something is terribly wrong with Colleen." Nora started to cry.

Emily willed it to be a bad dream, something that would go away when she opened her eyes. She'd wake up and think how strange that she had dreamed about the hospital when she had been at home, safe in her own bed.

"Emily, are you there?"

But it wasn't a nightmare or a dream. It was all too real.

Emily gripped the phone so hard she was vaguely surprised that it didn't break.

"Emily, Colleen's terribly sick. Please come down," Nora pleaded.

"On my way!" Emily cut the connection.

"Trouble?" Denise asked.

"Colleen is in the Emergency Room. Nora doesn't know what's wrong, just that she's ill. I have to go down. Denise, please cover for me. Everything has been taken care of except for talking to Cather, who should be Mr. Peters's new physician, and Coralie's meds." Emily hesitated, knowing full well that Denise would be within her rights to demand that she stay on the floor and simply call down for information about her daughter. It would have been a strict interpretation of hospital policy, and Emily would have been required to acquiesce unless she could find someone else to substitute for her.

"Go . . . And let us know what's happening, okay?"

Emily was out the door before Denise's words faded.

The fever. It had to be the fever. But the pediatrician had said it was only the flu. What had gone wrong? What could have happened?

Emily hit the doors to the Emergency Room and

ran to the desk. The nurse looked up and started to tell her that visitors must wait outside, then saw Emily's uniform and name tag.

"Mrs. Greer, your daughter is right over there in two," the nurse said, thawing slightly. "Doctor started an IV going before he was called away on another trauma. She's resting easily."

"How long before he's able to check her?"

"Could be an hour. You wouldn't *believe* the blood and gore back there! I wish people could find something else to do at night instead of carve and shoot each other up."

"An *hour*? But I thought this was an emergency! The way my friend talked, it's serious," Emily protested.

"I'm certain that it looks serious. But the doctor has done a quick check—that's why she's on the IV—and he'll finish up when everything else calms down. In the meantime, why don't you go in with her? Your friend is there, too."

Emily hurried into the room and then gasped as she caught sight of her daughter's face. Colleen was red and sweating. Her eyes were closed, and she had pulled her hands up over her chest in a defensive posture. Only the arm board she was tied to had kept the IV from being pulled out. Even in her sleep she was crying, moaning from the pain.

Nora stood beside the bed, looking miserable.

"How long has she been like this?" Emily asked as she felt Colleen's forehead. It was burning up.

"About an hour. I read until quite late, and then I went in to check her. She was moaning in her sleep, and it felt like her temperature had gone up. So I called your pediatrician. His service said he'd left for a trip and that the other doctor who was taking his calls was over at County and wouldn't be finished for a while. I wrapped her up and drove right here. I brought her in just as soon as I could, Emily."

Emily grabbed the thermometer and slipped a shield over the end. She placed it under Colleen's tongue and watched in horrified amazement as the digital display registered first 100, then 103, and finally 105.

"Oh, my God," she breathed. The child was going to go into convulsions if something wasn't done fast.

"Who's the doctor on ER duty?" Emily called out to the desk.

"Hemmil, but he's in with a knife wound to the gut, getting the man ready to be transferred up to OR, and then there's a gunshot wound right after that," the nurse said. "We're two physicians short—this damn flu has hit everyone. You know it's bad when doctors call in and they're so sick they're not making sense. We could insist that they come in, but who wants to be treated by someone who can't form a coherent sentence?"

"Who else do we have? We've got to get a doctor in here! This child is in real trouble," Emily cried. She tried to calm her own terror. It wouldn't do Colleen any good if her mother fainted from pure panic. She glanced anxiously over at her daughter. She didn't like the way Colleen was arching slightly backward, as if it hurt her to move her head forward. She was still moaning.

Emily had a terrible feeling it might be meningitis. She had seen that movement before, and it had never boded well for the patient.

"I could put out a call for the hospital, see who's in the building. But even that might not get someone in here," the nurse said doubtfully. "Have you checked her over? What's going on?" She walked into the room.

146

Emily showed the nurse the digital read-out on the thermometer, and then the pulse and blood pressure she had taken.

"That's not good," the nurse agreed. "I'll put out a call, see who we can drag in here. There's got to be a resident around who shouldn't be sleeping right now, anyway."

Emily waited. There was nothing else she could do.

"Nora, why don't you go out and get yourself a cup of coffee? I'll watch her," Emily said. Right now she didn't want to be with Nora or anyone else. She wanted only to be alone with Colleen until help arrived. And help had better come soon, Emily thought, or she was going to raise holy hell!

Emily waited until Nora had gone, and then began to check Colleen again. She couldn't just stand there. She had to do *something*. She tried to waken Colleen and got no response. The child's pupils were reacting sluggishly, and she didn't react to minor pain. Colleen was definitely in a coma—the only question was how deep and what was the cause. Emily still suspected meningitis. Then it dawned on her—there was no reason she couldn't do a couple of simple, quick tests to see if her diagnosis was right. She might be making a mistake, overreacting, like any other frightened mother.

"Okay, honey, let's give this the old Kernig's test, and we'll see if what Mommy thinks is wrong might actually *be* wrong," she said aloud.

Grimly Emily uncovered Colleen and touched her daughter's leg. She lifted it, flexing it at the hip and knee, then shifted the pressure, attempting to push the leg downward. Colleen moaned and fought, trying to keep her knee pulled up instead of letting it relax and stretch out of the bed.

"I was afraid of that," Emily whispered numbly.

Her child was lying here in a hospital bed with almost certain meningitis, and no one was doing anything. They were all involved with other cases, thinking Colleen could wait. But she *couldn't* wait! A child could die from meningitis. At the very least, she could be badly damaged. Wasn't Colleen Greer as important as a knife victim? Emily felt a sudden, unreasoning, white-hot anger. Her daughter was suffering, and no one cared!

"Someone said there was an emergency here?"

Emily's head snapped up. No! she thought dazedly. Of all the doctors she *didn't* want to see, she especially didn't want to see Dr. O'Shea, followed immediately by Dr. Shelby. They both looked rumpled, as if they'd been asleep. Maybe together?

"Oh, it's you, Greer. What are you doing, ignoring your patients upstairs to take care of some kid in Emergency? Isn't that frowned upon by your supervisor?"

Emily bit her lip to keep from screaming at the man. She loathed him, but she needed him. Colleen needed him.

"Dr. O'Shea, I am down here with Denise's permission. My daughter has a temp of one hundred five . . . ," Emily started to give the history.

O'Shea pushed past her, and Dr. Shelby followed. By the time they had crowded around the bed, Emily was almost at the door of the room.

O'Shea thumbed open Colleen's eyes and shone the light in them.

"Equal and reactive," he said briskly.

Emily choked back a cry. She knew Colleen's eyes were *not* equal and reactive. She'd tried it and there had been only a very slow reaction to light.

"What's her name?" O'Shea shot at Emily.

"Colleen," Emily's voice was wavering.

"Colleen! Colleen, can you hear me? Wake up!" O'Shea bellowed.

Colleen turned away from the sound, and moaned.

"Okay, verbal response a plus four. She's okay there."

Shelby dutifully wrote it down.

Emily couldn't believe what she was hearing. That wasn't a plus-four response. It was barely a plus two. The child had only moaned—she hadn't answered intelligibly. O'Shea was falsifying a report. Shelby's notes were going to state that Colleen had made a response that was only slightly incorrect. Emily's child was in severe distress, and this man was making up a record that bore no relation to Colleen's real reactions! It was like a horrible nightmare, and Emily couldn't wake up.

Dr. O'Shea placed his thumb against ridge of bone underneath Colleen's eyebrow and pressed hard. Emily could see the skin whitening and finally breaking. There was a crescent of blood where his thumbnail had penetrated.

"Stop it!" Emily yelled. "For God's sake, can't you see the child's in a coma?"

"Eye-opening, plus three," O'Shea ignored her.

Plus three—that meant that her eye-opening response had been spontaneous. The medical record would show that Dr. O'Shea had talked to Colleen and she had opened her eyes when he told her to.

"Okay motor response," O'Shea said.

Emily pushed her way to the surgeon and slid between him and her child.

"What do you think you're doing, Dr. O'Shea? Why are you building a record here that is so patently wrong that anyone reading it would say the child was only in mild distress?"

"I know what I'm doing, Greer. Get the hell out of

my way. You're just overreacting—a hysterical mother. I've seen them before, and I don't think much of them, whether they're nurses or not. My God, woman, you bring a kid in here with a mild case of the flu, and then fall apart when I don't immediately suspect she has meningitis or something equally as serious. You can't see her as she really is."

Emily was trembling with rage. This was the most unprofessional tirade she'd ever been subjected to in her life.

"As a nurse and as a mother, I'd like you to know that involvement of a family member does not automatically reduce a woman to a puddle of hysteria," she said, keeping her voice low and even.

O'Shea just looked at her.

Emily persisted. "I know my child is exhibiting all the symptoms of meningitis. *Look* at her, really check her. You'll realize I'm right!"

"You are hysterical. You can't even do a normal neuro check on her without finding something that isn't there," O'Shea said.

"I'll call another doctor," Emily said determinedly. "That record you are phonying up will look just fine in a court of law when another doctor says she has meningitis, won't it?"

For a moment she had a flash of déjà vu. She'd just been through this in a slightly different context with Peters. She had just seen a patient dumped for threatening to sue, and here she was, using the same ploy out of sheer desperation.

Shelby shouldered her to one side, away from Dr. O'Shea.

"Leave him alone, Greer. Haven't you figured out yet what happens when you fight with a doctor? It isn't healthy, is it?" Shelby said, smiling triumphantly. She liked the fear in Emily's eyes. This was what she had wanted all along—for Greer and that other nurse, Keith, to need Milton O'Shea and herself. Keith Jennings and Emily Greer were thorns in their collective side, and what did you do with thorns? You dug them out! This was a golden opportunity, a much better way to get revenge than anything they might have been able to devise.

But fury had replaced fear in Emily's eyes. "You are going to be hauled up in front of the medical-ethics board. You'll be taken into court. You'll never set foot in this hospital again if I have anything to say about it!" she hissed, pushing Shelby out of the way and confronting Dr. O'Shea.

"Get out of my way!" O'Shea grabbed Emily's arm and pulled her roughly to one side. His fingers bit into her skin, leaving crescents that matched the one above Colleen's eye.

The blast of bourbon on his breath caught Emily totally by surprise. Until that very moment, she hadn't connected the way Dr. O'Shea was behaving with anything other than simple meanness. But this —he never should have been in the hospital in such a condition, much less answering a call for a patient.

"Get out of here, and leave my daughter alone. I'll find someone else!" Emily pushed him away from Colleen. "*You are drunk!*"

"Don't even *say* such a thing!" Shelby cried. "Dr. O'Shea is not in any way impaired. It's *you*, Greer, can't you see that? *You're* the one causing all the problems here, and for no reason at all. It's the way you always act—cause trouble and then try to blame it on someone else, the doctor or the patient. Well, it won't work this time!" Shelby was almost screaming now. "Get out of his way and let him do his job. *Stop interfering!*"

Dr. Shelby grabbed Emily and threw her back

against the other table. Instruments scattered across the floor. Emily fell to her knees, momentarily dazed by the pain that knifed through her ribs. As she struggled back up, she looked at the door. Someone must have heard that. Someone should be coming in to check on what was happening. But what could she do? If O'Shea handed someone that phony report, it was possible they would dismiss Colleen without ever treating her. Her daughter was in a coma, and no one cared.

Emily was certain now that both doctors should have been locked up long ago. They had been feeding off each other's craziness, allowing themselves to pass beyond the bounds of reality. She could hardly run out into the middle of the Emergency receiving room and tell everyone that Dr. Shelby and Dr. O'Shea were crazy. They'd commit *her* before they'd listen. Still, she had to get help. Emily headed for the door, but Shelby was there before her.

"No, you're not going anywhere. You're going to wait while we finish here, and then you're going back upstairs while your daughter is taken back home." The woman almost crooned the words. It was like listening to someone straight out of the psych ward.

"You'll never get away with it," Emily said.

"Oh, but we will." The smell of bourbon on Shelby's breath was almost as strong as it was on O'Shea's. Alcohol was lending reality to their delusions. Surely they must realize that if they didn't treat Colleen here, Emily would find some other way to get competent medical care.

"Motor response, plus six," O'Shea said, as if he were totally unaware of the confrontation between Emily and Shelby. Shelby pushed Emily away again and wrote down the new figures.

Emily opened the door and slipped outside. She

could only hope and pray that neither of those two lunatics would do something catastrophic to her daughter while she was gone.

She ran over to the desk and grabbed the phone.

"What are you doing? What's going on in here?" A nurse came racing back from one of the other rooms and snatched the phone from Emily's hand "Please, you're a nurse, you know you can't just come in here and take over . . ."

"I'm *not* taking over! But I have to find Dr. Barnall. He's the only one who can help me!" Emily was so terrified that she was almost weeping. She had never thought that she might be putting her own daughter in danger by standing up for her rights and for refusing to take the blame for trouble that wasn't her fault.

"Dr. Barnall is up in surgery. Dr. O'Shea will take care of things. He's a good doctor, you know that. Surely you've worked with him," the nurse said, trying to soothe her.

Emily couldn't reply. What could she say? That he was trying to kill her child? They'd lock her up and wait for the staff psychiatrist to be called in, and by that time Colleen would be so damaged that she might never come out of this with any hope of being normal.

Oh, God! she thought. Colleen's hearing could be affected, as well as her eyes and her brain. Colleen could conceivably become deaf, blind, and mentally retarded, all because O'Shea needed to play God!

The door of the room opened, and Dr. Shelby and Dr. O'Shea came out. They cast triumphant glances at Emily, and Shelby slapped their report down on the desk.

"You can take it from here, nurse. The child is fine—just a case of the flu. We're recommending that she be taken home and given plenty of fluids. You know the routine. Nothing at all to worry about, just a mother who panics for no reason at all," O'Shea said grandly. Then he left, without filling out any of the forms or signing the report. Shelby trotted after him.

"Doctor . . . ," the nurse called after him, astonished. No doctor in his right mind would make recommendations and not back them up with all the paper work that accompanied a visit to the ER.

"*Now* what am I supposed to do?" the nurse said in disgust.

"You might try calling another doctor," Emily said between clenched teeth. "My daughter is still in there, and she has meningitis. I've done Kernig's on her, and it was positive. I *know* it's meningitis, but you'll never see it on the report those doctors have just written. If you doubt me, go in and run the test yourself. You'll see exactly the same things I saw. But remember, the longer you wait, the more damage there is going to be. And I promise you, if something serious happens because of Dr. O'Shea's inability to make a proper diagnosis, there is going to be hell to pay!"

"I'll call the Emergency Room doctor," the nurse decided.

"Why don't you do that?" Emily said grimly. "And at the same time, put in an emergency call for Dr. Barnall—or I'll do it myself. He has to see her. He's the chief neurosurgical resident."

"Go ahead and call him. I won't argue," the nurse said finally.

Chapter Eleven

Emily waited. Dr. Hemmil, the Emergency Room doctor, checked Colleen, and left after ordering a lumbar puncture. He had put in a call himself to Terry Barnall to perform the procedure and to take over the case, and had also ordered a drip of two kinds of antibiotics through the IV that had already been established. Emily had winced when she heard the order for the lumbar puncture. She knew how painful the procedure could be. On the other hand, she was almost certain that Colleen wouldn't feel anything she was too sick.

Emily sat beside Colleen's bed now, holding her hand and talking quietly to her about anything that came into her head. Emily had taken some alcohol out of the Emergency Room cabinet, and kept sponging her daughter down periodically, trying to bring the fever below 103. As she worked, she talked. She had learned long ago that patients in a coma did indeed hear everything that went on around them, and she had no intention of frightening Colleen by weeping over her or carrying on. Instead, she talked about the drawing Colleen had brought home from school a few days ago, and the tree in their yard that was blossoming already, promising a good harvest of the peaches that Colleen liked. Occasionally she sang snatches of songs.

Time and again, she closed her hand around her daughter's fingers, just to have the comfort of her touch. Colleen was still hot, and she moaned every few minutes, but at least now she would be cared for by someone who agreed with Emily that the child was terribly ill.

"Mrs. Greer?" The ER nurse came into the room, holding the papers Dr. O'Shea and Dr. Shelby had written out.

"What is it?"

"I wanted to know if you want these papers. It seems to me that the only doctor who really checked your daughter has been Hemmil—he's the one who did the initial consult and then came back and ordered all the drugs. . . ." The nurse looked at her hopefully. It was obvious what she was thinking—if they crumpled up those papers and threw them away, there would be no need for any kind of action. If, on the other hand, the papers were entered into Colleen's chart, it was certain that a medical review would be called in on the case.

"Put them in the chart. And I'd like copies of all of them, too," Emily said coolly. She wasn't going to let this be swept under the rug.

"All right, if you're sure . . . " the nurse said.

"I am positive," Emily stated.

The door banged open again, and Terry Barnall,

still in his surgical greens, hurried into the room. He glanced from Emily to Colleen.

"What happened?"

Emily resisted the urge to throw herself into his arms, rest her head on his shoulder, and let him comfort her. She was amazed at the need she felt to have him hold her close.

Gulping back a sob of relief, she tersely outlined Colleen's symptoms and what Dr. Hemmil had done, omitting the almost surreal encounter with O'Shea and Shelby. She would discuss that with him later.

"Okay, first things first. We'll get that lumbar puncture, then run the tests."

Emily looked at Colleen and winced.

"She's positive on Kernig, and she's got the drugs going now—couldn't she do without the lumbar?" She was asking as a mother, not as a trained nurse. But the thought of her daughter going through that procedure was almost more than she could bear.

Terry shook his head. "I suspect that we've got a *Haemophilus influenzae* going here. The tests will give me an exact answer, and then we'll have an idea of what drug will work on that nasty little bug. Then we'll discontinue one or the other of the antibiotics. And if it turns out that the bug is resistant to *both* the ones she's on right now, we'll try her on one of the cephalosporins. All of this is in answer to a question that I know you asked because you love Colleen and don't want to see her hurt. But the point is, Emily, I don't dare fly by the seat of my pants. I've got to have that cerebral-spinal fluid to culture."

Emily nodded. She had feared that would be the answer, but she didn't have to like it.

"Sometimes knowing what's going on is worse than simply coming into a hospital and handing everything over to the doctor, trusting him to make the right decisions, isn't it?" Terry walked over to Emily and put his arms around her. He held her for a few moments.

"Thank you, Terry," Emily finally said. She felt better for having had the touch of a warm and caring human being.

"Okay—now the big question. You can be in here when we do the test. Some parents like to be close for moral support. Do you want to stay with Colleen?" Terry asked as one of the ER nurses rolled in a cart with the lumbar-puncture tray on it, packed in bulky blue sterile wrapping.

Terry watched Emily as she looked at the cart and gulped hard. He recognized that look of absolute horror.

"On the other hand," he added hastily, "you just might want to go out there and wait. Frankly, with Colleen the way she is right now, I don't think she's going to feel a thing. But it has to be done, and soon. She's got to be taken upstairs and into the Pediatric Intensive Care Unit."

Terry took Emily's hands and pulled her close again. "It's all right, Emily. You aren't deserting Colleen just because you can't bring yourself to be in the room with her when she goes through this. You know I'll take the best care of her that I know how, and I know a pretty fair amount about these things."

Emily found it hard to tear her eyes away from the cart with the kit sitting on it. She'd been present before during these procedures, but it had never been *her* little girl before. She was glad Terry understood how she felt.

"I vote for outside. I'll go tell Nora what's going on—she's my housemate. She went out for coffee about forty-five minutes ago—maybe she's in the waiting room."

158

"Good idea. I'll come right out the instant we're done," Terry said. He kissed her once on the mouth, and then turned away. Emily's lips seemed to tingle. She took comfort from that brief kiss, and most of all from the compassion Terry had shown.

She leaned over and passed the kiss on to Colleen, feeling the heat of her daughter's skin as she did so. Colleen would never remember any of this, and for that Emily was profoundly grateful.

"Mrs. Greer, you wanted a copy of these reports?" another nurse called to her, holding out a sheaf of papers as Emily left the room.

"Thank you," Emily said. She took the papers and stuffed them into her pocket. Later, there would be plenty of time to decide what to do about O'Shea and Shelby.

Emily walked through the swinging doors and found Nora in the waiting room along with dozens of other people who were ready to be treated when there was a doctor available.

Nora jumped up and came over to Emily.

"How is she? Do I take her back home? Was I wrong to bring her in?"

Emily put an arm around her friend. "It's meningitis. They're doing a lumbar right now. And you saved her life by bringing her in. If you hadn't, she probably would have died."

Nora didn't know what to say. To think the poor kid had something as serious as meningitis!

"What happens now?" she said at last.

Emily sank into one of the few empty chairs. "We wait until Dr. Barnall has done the lumbar puncture, and then he'll have Colleen moved up to Peds. She'll be here in the hospital for a while."

Emily looked up at Nora. Her face was drawn, and her clothes were rumpled, as if she'd thrown them on without thinking. Her hands were beginning to tremble. Emily hadn't had time to think about how tired her friend must be. Nora had worked all day and then taken care of Colleen all night. It was almost four, and she still hadn't been home to rest.

"Go home, Nora. I'm sorry—I just wasn't thinking about you. I'll let you know what happens here," Emily said, taking Nora's hand.

"But you need a friend to be with you right now," Nora protested.

"Yes, I need a friend, and you're the best friend I could possibly want, but I know what's going to happen from here on in. This is my territory—it holds no terrors for me, like it might for some of these other people." Emily waved a hand toward the room filled with frightened, injured, and tired men and women. "Colleen's going to be all right. I know Dr. Barnall will take excellent care of her, and she'll also get the best of care in Pediatric ICU. So go—you have to get some rest if you're even going to attempt to make it into work tomorrow."

Nora was about to protest again, but she was cut short by a long yawn. She laughed apologetically. "I guess you're right. But are you certain?"

"I'm positive. Get going." Emily stood up. "Where are you parked?"

"Right outside the door," Nora answered.

"I'll walk out with you and wait until you're safely inside. Then you get right on home and sleep."

Emily had to wait only a few minutes after she returned before Terry Barnall came back out, holding a tube in his hand.

"Terry?" she said anxiously, going over to him.

"Come with me, Emily. I'm hand-carrying this up to the lab." He looked worried.

160

Emily looked at the tube and whistled. The spinal fluid was milky, as opposed to the normal slightly yellowish clear fluid.

"That's one hell of a bad infection, isn't it?" she said softly.

"I won't lie to you. Yes, it is. If there had been any more delay, I don't know what might have happened. Thank heavens your friend brought Colleen in immediately instead of waiting. As it is, I think we'll be able to avoid most of the long-term effects."

"You mean my daughter won't be blind, deaf, or mentally retarded?" Emily asked bitterly.

"I *hope* it won't happen. I *think* it won't happen," Terry said. "I'm doing everything I can, okay?"

"I know, Terry. And thank you. Someday soon I'll tell you what happened in there before you came down from surgery. You're not going to believe it!"

He stopped outside the lab.

"Why don't you go on up to Peds ICU? I'll meet you there, and then once you're certain that Colleen's fine, you can go back to work—if you feel like it. But I have to see you before you set foot on Six again." Terry leaned forward and kissed her again. He realized that he was suddenly feeling very protective toward this woman, and it was a strange sensation. He had spent his whole adult life avoiding emotional entanglements. Now he'd apparently stepped right into the middle of one and he didn't even mind.

Emily gazed after Terry as he walked through the door to the lab. She didn't understand what the hell was going on, but she liked it. The most they'd ever done was have breakfast together with a sick kid in the other room, and yet he had kissed her twice.

Maybe it doesn't mean anything at all, Emily thought as she took the elevator up to Pediatrics. Whatever the kisses meant or didn't mean, the analysis was going to have to wait until she had the situation with Colleen under control. Then she'd go home, pour a stiff drink, and think about it.

"Mrs. Greer?" the nurse at the Peds desk called to her as she stepped off the elevator.

"Yes?"

"We were expecting you. Colleen's already in the ICU down the hall, and the nurses would like to talk to you. Dr. Barnall will be coming up shortly."

"Thank you," Emily said. She was surprised that the nurse had been watching for her. Then she remembered that she herself always kept an eye out for her patients' families. If someone didn't take them in hand, they could walk for hours, roaming through the hospital, too distraught to ask specific directions to the patient's room.

Peds was a new floor for Emily, and she was glad to see that the children were surrounded by bright colors and shapes and textures that would please them even when they were sick. She moved the curtain aside that marked the entrance of the Intensive Care Unit, and walked into a room full of machines whose hums and noises mirrored all too realistically the adult ICU. Neither the balloons and rainbows on the walls, nor the beds covered with bright red-and-blue blankets instead of the regulation hospital white disguised the fact that this was a place where very sick kids were desperately trying to hang on to life.

"Colleen's over there." The nurse gestured toward one of the beds that were arranged in a semicircle around the nurses' station so the nurses had visual access to each child all the time.

"We've got her on a heart monitor, and she's receiving cephalosporins right now. Her temp is down to one hundred three which is really good. It's a solid drop from her admitting temp downstairs."

Emily walked over to her daughter.

"Hey, honey, Mommy's here," she said softly. There was a flicker of the eyelids, but Emily couldn't be certain that it was in response to her voice. Her heart contracted in pain as she looked at the little girl. When Colleen was healthy and running around the house, she seemed to fill the room where she was with noise and laughter and explosions of interest. Here, lying silently on the bed, Emily realized just how tiny and fragile her daughter really was, and it tore at her. Colleen was too young to have the light and sound of the world, the dancing and the colors taken away from her. Would she lose the music she loved to play and sing, the songs she listened to over and over on the radio? It was possible, Emily knew, and there was nothing at all she could do about it. A feeling of total despair washed over her, and the hot tears that had been waiting all night to fall suddenly poured down her cheeks.

"I know." The nurse had come up beside her silently and handed Emily a tissue, then waited until Emily had dried her eyes. "It's bad when you know what's going on. But Dr. Barnall is the best you could get. He'll do everything in his power to help Colleen, and so will we."

Emily nodded.

"Is her father going to be coming in? We like to know whom to expect on the night shift. With most new admissions at this time of night, only one parent may stay with the child during the wee hours."

Emily started guiltily. She hadn't thought about contacting Nicholas. She had concentrated so hard on Colleen that she had forgotten his existence.

Emily turned stricken eyes to the nurse. "I have to confess, I haven't even called him."

"Oh . . ." It was clear that the nurse was wondering what kind of marriage this was, when a woman could neglect to call the father of her child when something went terribly wrong.

"Would you like to use the phone in the parents' room? It's just across the hall, and at this time of night it's pretty quiet."

"I wish I didn't have to tell him at all," Emily fretted aloud. "The middle of the night isn't the best time to try and talk to Nicholas." Then she wished she hadn't voiced her thoughts—she usually didn't allow anyone to know just how bad things were between her ex-husband and herself.

The nurse hesitated. "That's your decision, of course. But if you *do* want to call him, the phone's in there."

Emily stood beside Colleen's bed for almost thirty minutes more. She knew she should be getting back upstairs to take over her patients, but at the moment she couldn't have played nurse to anyone else. She was only a mother right now, a frightened, angry, and unhappy mother. She didn't want to even think about medications and changing IVs and listening to the patients talk about how they felt. Her daughter needed her.

But she had to call Nicholas. She had put it off as long as she could. Colleen was his daughter, too, even though he hadn't shown a bit of interest in her since the divorce.

Emily reluctantly left Colleen and walked over to the parents' room. It was quiet, with low lighting and warm colors intended to soothe mothers and fathers who were worried and sick at heart about their children. She dialed Nicholas's number and waited for the answering service to refer her call through the maze of instructions that Nicholas had left about never being interrupted during his free time.

"I'm sorry, Mrs. Greer, but Mr. Greer asks that you call back later in the morning and speak to his secretary," the woman at the answering service said, her voice carefully neutral.

"Get Mr. Greer back on the line and tell him that his daughter almost died tonight! Is he interested, or would he rather not be bothered?" Emily snapped.

She heard the sharp intake of breath from the woman on the other end of the line. There was a brief interval of silence while she relayed the message, and then Nicholas's voice boomed at her.

"What the hell is this, Emily? Do you know what time it is? You'd better not have cooked this damned excuse as a way to find out about your money, or I swear you'll never see a penny of it!" Nicholas was always loud and nasty-tempered when he was awakened from a sound sleep.

"Colleen is in the Pediatric Intensive Care Unit at Ridge. She has meningitis. They've got her on antibiotics and she's had a lumbar puncture," Emily said, surprised that her voice sounded as steady as it did. She heard a noise behind her, and looked up to see Terry Barnall standing in the doorway. He looked exhausted, there were dark shadows under his eyes, his lab coat was wrinkled, and his tie was twisted to one side.

"Is she going to be all right?" Nicholas asked, still yelling. "How could you let her get so sick?"

Emily closed her eyes in irritation. How could she have stayed married to this man for so many years? Had she been secretly into masochism?

"I didn't *let* her get sick! I hope and pray she'll be okay. She's under a very good doctor's care and we'll just have to wait and see."

"Well, why did you wake me up in the middle of the night to tell me this? Why didn't you wait until you found out something definite?"

Emily gasped in shock. She hadn't expected him to be friendly, but she *had* thought he might be concerned. In the background, she could hear a woman's voice questioning him querulously about the phone call. She said something about it disturbing her children.

"I called because I had the misguided feeling that you might want to know that your daughter is in the hospital, and damn near died. But of course, I forgot—you have Maureen and her two kids to occupy your time, and that's fine with me. But you've gone a little too far this time, Nicholas." Emily slammed the receiver down.

"Trouble?" Terry asked.

Emily sighed. "Not really. I'm just wondering how a man could know that his child is in the hospital with a serious illness and just not give a damn about it. And then the thought occurs to me that I should have known—I was married to Nicholas. I knew what he was like."

"He never did care about her?"

"Not really. Nicholas gave most of his time to his career. Colleen and I grabbed whatever spare moments we could, but mostly we were left on our own."

"He's a fool! There's nothing in the world like a family to come home to. I can't tell you how lonely my apartment seems sometimes, with just me and the geraniums. I'm looking forward to having a wife and lots of kids and noise and laughter. . . ." Terry suddenly stopped talking and looked distinctly uncomfortable. Apparently he had revealed more of himself than he had meant to.

Emily began to cry again.

"Hey, Emily, I'm sorry. That was thoughtless of me. I know how much it must hurt you to have him turn his back on Colleen that way. And I think he's a damn fool, giving up such a darling little girl and such a wonderful woman." Terry strode over to Emily and folded her in his arms. After holding her for a few minutes, he reached over and grabbed some tissues from one of the boxes that had been placed around the room at strategic points. Almost every parent who visited this room ended up having a good cry before they left.

Emily blew her nose and looked up at him. She smiled, though her smile was a little wobbly around the edges.

"I'm okay. You know, you have a way about you like no other man I've ever known. I'm glad to have you for a friend." She didn't notice the peculiar expression that passed over Terry's face when she said the word "friend."

"Oh, I almost forgot—I have a present for you, one that's going to remind you of me every single time you go to the bathroom." Terry handed her a small vial of pills and laughed at the astonished look on her face.

"Rifampin?" Emily asked. She knew exactly what he meant when he said she'd think of him every time she went to the bathroom—Rifampin colored the urine a brilliant orange.

"I think you need it. Normally I wouldn't order a prophylactic antimicrobial treatment, but you're in close contact with patients every day and with Colleen, and I'd hate to see you get sick. It's a very slim chance, but you could be carrying something. Better to be overcautious than to fight an outbreak of meningitis on Ridge Six, don't you think?"

"Right, as usual. And come to think of it, I'd better call Denise and tell her what's happened to Colleen. She may not want me back on the floor for a few days, anyway, just to be safe."

Terry's beeper began to go off, cutting into their conversation.

"Hell, someone else just came into Emergency! I'll give a run by Colleen and then head on down. I'll be talking to you in the next few hours, though." Terry leaned over and brushed his lips over her cheek, then ran out the door, his stethoscope bouncing wildly.

Emily sat down. As she did, she heard the papers crinkle in the pocket of her uniform. She took them out, smoothed them, and read again the reports that O'Shea and Shelby had prepared, reports that, had they been believed, would have condemned her daughter to death or severe damage.

There was something . . . Emily struggled to remember. Something about reporting things like this, but not to the hospital. . . .

Keith—that was who had talked to her about it! She remembered him telling her about his friend and the series of articles he planned to do about the discriminatory treatment of patients. Maybe he'd be interested in the treatment some doctors gave nurses when they stood up for their own rights.

Emily picked up the white in-house phone and placed a call to Ridge Six East. She spoke for a few moments to Denise, telling her about Colleen, the meningitis, and the Rifampin. Denise, she was glad to hear, agreed that a few days off would be in the best interests of Emily's patients as well as herself.

"So it's settled—I'll take a week off and then I'll

come back to work if Colleen is well enough to be looked after by my friend Nora at night," Emily said. "Now, one last question. Is Keith around the nurses' station so I could talk to him?"

Denise turned away from the phone and called Keith. A moment later, he picked up the receiver.

"Emily—sorry to hear about your kid. Do you want something from me?" he asked. It was obvious from his tone of voice that he was in a hurry.

"I need to know the phone number of the man who's writing the series on Ridge. He might like to know what happens when doctors have it in for a nurse who disagrees with them. That discrimination might have resulted in the death of a child."

"Any proof?"

"Would doctors' notes that were written but left unsigned do? If you had to prove that it wasn't a forgery, a handwriting expert could do a lot with these pages," Emily said.

"Sounds like a winner. Let me give you Bill's number."

Within a few hours, Bill Sonderson would have some startling new information for his series.

Chapter Twelve

"Please, please don't do that!" The voice wavered with pain and confusion. "Tommy . . ."

Keith looked up from the syringe he was preparing for Cynda Arden. That sounded like Coralie Cooper's voice, and it seemed to be coming from her room.

"Please, Tommy . . . ," the cry came again, and then the sound of someone shushing her.

Keith hurried to finish with the syringe, then slipped it into his pocket. He'd get to Cynda in a minute. Something was going on in Coralie's room, and he didn't like the sound of it.

Keith's rubber-soled shoes didn't make a sound as he approached. He stopped for a moment outside the door and listened to see if he'd identified the source correctly.

"Okay, Grandma, where did you put it this time? I know you have the check, because it was supposed to come in the day you came to the hospital. Come on, give it to me. How else do you expect me and my mom to pay the bills?" The voice was that of a male teenager with a slightly whining, nasal quality. Keith disliked him immediately, even without seeing the kid.

Coralie answered, "You and your mother didn't make the mortgage payment last month. I know because I got a letter about it. What do you want me to do, lose the house because you take the money and fritter it away on fun and games? Did you and your mother actually expect that a mortgage payment could be missed and no one would tell me?" Coralie's voice was slightly stronger now.

"Hell, we don't care if you take the Social Security check, that's all right. But you can't have the annuity check from Grandpa, too. Mom says that was meant for my dad, and it should have come to her when Dad died. You're cheating us by taking all of it. You never think about us." Tommy was wheedling now. "We'll make up the money that didn't get paid last month. We promise, okay?"

"No! I'm not giving either of you the check. First of all, what ever gave your mother the idea that Grandpa left that money to your dad? That annuity was bought with money that your grandfather and I earned."

Coralie's voice increased in volume, overriding her grandson's whining. "Let me tell you, it was no picnic traveling around the country in that van, working the small-time carnies and circuses. I read more people's palms than you'd ever believe. And we saved almost every cent of our earnings. I wanted to make sure that when we found the place where we wanted to settle down, we'd have the money to do it. It meant missed meals, doing without, and trying to keep a fifteen-year-old truck alive to haul our wooden van to the next town. When we bought the house, we had a little money left over, and it went into the annuity. It wasn't meant for your father, it was meant for my old age."

"But you gave the money from that annuity to Dad."

Coralie stopped the boy. "The only reason your family ever saw a cent of it is because my poor son needed it—he had a hard time keeping a job. But it wasn't *meant* for your father. It was *my* money that I let him use!" Coralie was obviously angry. "And as for giving it to you, why should I? I've given you money in the past, and you and your mother just fritter it away. When I trust you two to make payments on a house, or on the car, you take the money and spend it on other things instead. No, Tommy, I will not give it to you." Keith heard Coralie thump the bed with her free arm. "Do you understand? Nothing will change my mind. I told you that last week when you came in here, high on something, and demanded the money then."

Keith had heard enough to make his blood boil. To begin with, there shouldn't have been anyone in that room at this time of night. No visitors were allowed in the hospital after nine in the evening except in extreme cases. Coralie wasn't an emergency case.

"No! Damn it, Tommy, give me that back . . ."

There was a dull thud, and then a shrill, high-pitched scream from Coralie.

Keith burst into the room and caught Tommy's arm as the young man swung downward again, his clenched fist hitting Coralie's arm that was immobilized by the IV board.

Keith was taller by almost a foot and about a hundred pounds heavier than the teenager, and he

173

used every ounce of that weight to bring the boy's arm to a stop. Suddenly there were two people screaming in pain.

"Coralie. Coralie, it's all right—it's me. I've stopped him," Keith said, never loosening his grip on the young man's arm.

But it was obvious that she couldn't hear him. She was crying, her face crumpled and wet from tears of pain and fright.

There was no time for niceties, even if it was the middle of the night. Keith hit the intercom, ringing a buzzer at the nurses' desk.

"Trouble?" Denise was instantly on the line.

"Trouble. Get security up here stat. And send for a portable X ray. We've got one broken arm that needs to be done for Coralie Cooper, and another for some young punk named Tommy."

Denise didn't stop to ask questions. Within two minutes, three security guards were in the room to take over with Tommy. The young man was blubbering with pain, and he didn't look nearly so mean when his lips quivered and he couldn't stop the tears.

"What happened?" one of the guards asked, indicating that Keith could loosen his grip on the boy's arm. There were two cops between Tommy and the door, and from the looks of him, he wasn't about to go anywhere in any hurry.

"Caught him in here beating up on his grandmother. Seems he wanted a check she was hiding in this pillow . . ." Keith reached inside the pillowcase and found it empty. He swung around and glared at Tommy.

"I suggest that you give him a pat-down, and just make certain that the envelope you're going to find in one of his pockets makes it back into his grandmother's hands," Keith said, his fists clenched. He'd have loved to work the little bastard over and finish up the fight with a good kick in the rear for good measure.

"Sure thing," the cop said, and began to pat down Tommy in the most violent manner possible. In the interest of a good, solid search, he jostled Tommy's arm and pulled the jacket back, twisting it slightly. He knew just when to stop so there wasn't too much more damage done to the arm. He did, however, place an occasional thumb to a pressure point. By the time the security cop had retrieved the check from the back pocket of Tommy's jeans, the boy was almost groveling on the floor, writhing in pain.

"X ray?"

"Right in here," Keith said, and then blanched. In all the excitement, he'd forgotten to alert Dr. Mendelsohn. He'd overstepped his bounds in even suggesting that an X ray be taken on the arm without consulting the doctor.

"Wait just a minute, please," Keith asked and hurried out to the phone to call Dr. Mendelsohn. He had the doctor on the line in a matter of seconds.

"Looks like it's the third or fourth night in a row for you, Doctor. And I'm sorry about it. I just found out what happened to Coralie Cooper's leg, but unfortunately not soon enough to stop the same thing from happening to her arm. I'm to blame for that—I just didn't move fast enough. . . ."

"Hold on, and I'll be right there. Then you can fill me in. Get an X ray and have it ready to show me the instant I walk through that door," Mendelsohn said. "And make certain that she has an injection immediately for any pain."

Keith was relieved. He was sure he wouldn't have to explain a small discrepancy in time for the X rays.

Keith put down the phone and looked up just in time to see Tommy being hauled away.

"Lady says she'll prefer charges of assault and battery. We'll have the city police up to see her in a while," a guard said.

"Better check with me before you send anyone up. Dr. Mendelsohn has ordered some pain medications and she's likely to be zonked for a while." Keith hesitated and looked over at Tommy.

"He's probably got a broken arm. Get him downstairs, and they can take care of it in Emergency."

The guard smiled nastily. "I might just develop a hangnail and ask to be seen first."

Keith gave him the thumbs-up sign, then went back into the room with the syringe filled with Demerol. "Coralie, honey, please look at me."

The X-ray technician stepped back. She hadn't received orders yet from Keith to take the pictures and had been waiting for Coralie to acknowledge that she was there, and to allow her to touch the arm.

Gradually the old woman raised her head and met Keith's eyes.

"Hey, Coralie, what's my pretty lady doing crying like that? I know that arm hurts, but you're sobbing as if your heart was broken, too. . . ." Keith knew that was exactly what the matter was.

"Damn that Tommy and his no-good mother, too! I should have thrown out my son and that wife of his when he walked into the house with her the first time! I knew she was trouble from the minute I laid eyes on her, with her tight jeans and no bra and chewing and popping her gum all over the place. Real trash," Coralie said fiercely.

"That's the spirit," Keith said, laughing. He had been worried that she would retreat into that distant place where some old people go when they're hurt. Sometimes, Keith knew, they never came back.

Keith looked at Coralie's left arm. At least if

something had to happen, it was lucky to be on an arm already splinted with the IV board.

"Okay, Coralie, I'm going to have the tech over there take a picture. We're not going to move it at all, except to lay it flat on the surface here, if you can."

Coralie started to move the arm.

"Whoa, I didn't mean move it right yet! Just keep it where it is now, and show me on the back of the board where you think the break is," Keith instructed her.

"I can feel bones grating, right about here," Coralie said, indicating a spot almost at her wrist.

Keith bit his lip. She really should move it, in order to get the best picture. But he'd hate to cause any further damage.

"Is the board holding it really steady? Can you move it without too much pain?"

Coralie tried and winced.

"Okay, that's it then. We'll just take it where it lays. Come on over here." Keith motioned to the X-ray technician.

"My name is Mary," she said coolly.

"I know. It's been Mary for all the years that I've been here," Keith soothed her. "Now take a pretty picture, will you, Mary dear? Dr. Mendelsohn will be here any second, and he expects to have them hanging over there in front of the light so he can see what he has to do."

Mary grumphed and then settled down to taking the X rays. She was a wizard at getting the best pictures from the worst angles. She knew what she was doing and was always sent out on the hard cases. This was definitely one of the hardest. Keith left the room while the pictures were being taken—hospital rules mandated that anyone who wasn't bedridden leave while the machine was in use.

"Give me a minute, and these will be in your hands," Mary said to Dr. Mendelsohn as he walked into the room.

While they waited, Keith filled in the doctor on the story behind the injuries Coralie had sustained.

"I suggest that we have someone from social services come up and talk to her tomorrow," he said. "Coralie needs help in keeping these moochers away from her. There's no reason in the world why she should have to worry about being beaten up so that someone can steal her checks. She needs protection."

"I'll write orders for it. In the meantime . . ." Dr. Mendelsohn reached for the X rays that Mary brought back, and shoved them into the holder at the top of the light. He flipped the switch and looked at the bones that had been clearly outlined. Mary had lived up to her reputation once again. Even from the worst possible angle, and with other bones in Coralie's body that could have gotten in the way, Dr. Mendelsohn was able to see all too clearly the break above Coralie's wrist.

He sighed heavily.

"Call the casting room, and we'll take her down. It's going to be simple to set—from the looks of it, it's only moved slightly out of position thanks to that board. But it's going to slow up her recovery even more. Damn it, doesn't that little bastard care that old people don't heal fast? He could have caused damage that would put her in a nursing home instead of in her own place, with her things around her that she loves. How is she going to put in her garden. . . ." Dr. Mendelsohn stopped abruptly and looked over his glasses at Keith.

Keith nodded. Coralie had managed to catch Dr. Mendelsohn in her web, too. The old woman charmed everyone who came in contact with her—everyone, that is, except her daughter-in-law and grandson.

"Hell of a world, isn't it?" Mendelsohn sighed.

Keith felt something poking the side of his leg, and reached into his pocket.

"Oh, damn," he breathed. He'd been so intent on what was happening with Coralie that he'd completely forgotten about Cynda. And there was her medication, right there in his pocket, just waiting for her.

He ran down the hall, avoiding other nurses by inches as he rushed into her room.

Cynda was lying on her back. She looked even more fragile than she had the day before. Her skin seemed almost translucent, and she had barely enough energy to raise her arm and salute him. For the first time that Keith could remember, she wasn't doing anything. She didn't have a book open to read, there was no sewing ready for the next stitch, and none of the computer games she liked to play were humming or beeping.

"Cynda, honey, I'm sorry—we had quite a dust-up down the hall. Ready for your injection?"

Cynda nodded. She didn't have enough breath left to answer him.

Swiftly Keith gave her the medication and then took her arm, feeling her pulse and noting with dismay that her skin was progressively becoming colder.

Frowning, Keith motioned for Cynda to roll over as far as she could so he could listen to her chest. He moved the stethoscope and listened again. There was almost no air moving. Keith had given her a treatment just an hour before, yet there had been no improvement.

Quickly he set up the oxygen mask, fitting the

elastic over her ears, and turned on the silver spigot at the wall. He waited until he heard the hiss and then read the dial. The pressure was fine—everything was flowing.

"Damn it, I should have been here," he muttered. Coralie had been important, but he should have asked someone to take over with Cynda. He'd just plain forgotten her. The thought gave him great pain. He'd never knowingly do anything to hurt any patient, least of all someone like Cynda.

"Keith, I don't—feel—very—good . . . ," Cynda managed to say. Every word cost her an immense effort. She struggled to catch her breath between each syllable.

Lara Mendoza had come over and was standing silently by her bed. It was the first time she had ever seen someone as sick as Cynda, and it shook her to her core. There she lay, a girl twenty-two years old, and she could be dying. Lara was stunned. Until now, death had been mostly an abstraction.

"I'll be right back, okay? Hang in there, kid—we'll get help!" Keith dashed out of the room. He probably should have stayed with Cynda, but he didn't want her to hear what he had to say to the doctor.

Within moments he had alerted Dr. Shelby to the crisis, taking the orders for the blood gases, for a respiratory therapist, and for a transport up to Intensive Care. Once in the ICU, there would be other tests, and the fight to keep Cynda Arden alive would begin in earnest.

"I'll be there immediately," Dr. Shelby's voice was cold. She hated working with Keith.

Keith raced back to the room and checked on Cynda again. She was a little more responsive with the oxygen but she still couldn't talk easily and she lay back against the bed, not moving, not seeming to be aware of the people around her.

"Come on, Cynda!" Lara was saying as Keith came in. "You've still got one more quilt to do! Look, you've got all the material here, ready to go. You can't give up on that. What would the twins think when they realized that their very own aunt only finished one quilt? Imagine the fights they'd have over it. And weren't you just telling me how great it was to finally know that you had twin nieces? And then there are your finals—how are you going to keep your grades up if you miss those exams? You told me your game plan, and it sure didn't involve getting this sick. . . ."

Lara's voice almost broke, but she got it under control. She was holding Cynda's hand tightly, and the contact seemed to comfort them both.

Keith didn't disturb them. Instead, he busied himself with packing the various books, games, and sewing projects into the plastic bags that were given to all patients for their belongings. The bags would be tagged and sent up with Cynda to the ICU, where they would be kept in a locker until her family could retrieve them or she was sent back down to six, or one of the other floors.

The respiratory therapist and the transport arrived almost at the same time. There was a flurry of activity, and then Cynda was gone on her way to another place where her fight against the killer disease would continue. Keith knew there was no guarantee that she would win.

Chapter Thirteen

"Well, look who's back on the floor and all ready for a pain injection!"

Emily walked into the room and theatrically threw open her arms, as if she were really welcoming Mr. Peters back to Six East. Both of them knew better.

"So, are you ready to torture me again?" Peters said, eyeing her balefully.

"I certainly am. You're my first patient on my first night back after some time off. And just think—I get to give you a pain injection right off the bat. Couldn't ask for anything better than that!"

Peters scowled at her. "What were you off for? You didn't have that horrible flu that's going around, did you? I don't want to get that. I can't think of anything worse than getting a horrible cold and sneezing and joggling this cast around. At least this new doctor seems to have repaired things right this time. Hardly any pain so far, at least not like it was." Peters gave his cast a thump.

"No, it wasn't the flu. It was my daughter. She was here in the hospital with meningitis," Emily said. "And no, you can't catch it from me."

Peters looked at her, surprised. "She was here? What was her name—Colleen? Nicholas's kid?"

"I only have one daughter, and, yes, her name is Colleen."

"Funny," Peters said, "I didn't hear anything about her being in the hospital."

"There was no reason you should have. Nurses don't gossip with patients about other nurses' private lives."

Peters nodded slowly. "When did she go home?"

"Two days ago," Emily said. She couldn't imagine why Leopold Peters would show even mild curiosity about Colleen. He had done everything in his power to make certain the child didn't receive a penny of support from her father. It was ironic that he should be interested in her well-being now.

But Emily didn't have time to stand around and wonder about Leopold Peters. There were other patients to care for, and other work to do.

"One injection coming up," Emily said cheerfully. She cleaned, stabbed, and rubbed in one swift movement.

It was a shame, she thought as she always did, that she couldn't make it hurt more. She would have liked to give Mr. Attorney Peters a *real* pain in the ass one of these days!

"With Colleen in the hospital, I'd imagine you've spoken to Nicholas at least a couple of times. How did things go between the two of you when he came to visit Colleen? Or did he work it so that you weren't there at the same time?"

Emily took a deep breath. He wanted to know how she and Nicholas got along? He should know! He was the one who had advised Nicholas never to talk to her, except through an attorney. Peters was the one who had encouraged Nicholas to cut off any communication at all with his daughter, and now he dared ask her how she had gotten along with her ex-husband, who hadn't even cared enough about Colleen to come to the hospital! She wondered how fast she would be fired for actually taking a swing at a patient. She imagined she'd be out of a job within ten minutes. Only the stack of unpaid bills at home kept her from acting on her first instinct.

"We didn't see each other," was all she said.

"Then he *did* time the visits to stay away from you. Good. I'd have hated to have you taking potshots at each other over the kid's bed."

"I didn't say that," Emily said quietly. She was gritting her teeth.

"Yes, you did," Peters answered testily.

"I did *not* say that Nicholas and I avoided each other. How could we avoid each other when he never, not once, not for five minutes, set foot in this hospital to visit his own child? Nicholas didn't care whether she lived or died!" Emily said and marched out of the room.

For the first time in many years, Leopold Peters was shocked into silence. He'd seen almost everything in his long and varied career, but he'd never actually known a parent before who could completely and irrevocably cut a small child out of his life without ever looking back.

Emily didn't see the expression on Leopold Peters's face turn to fury as he thought about Nicholas Greer's callousness. It was even more reprehensible, Peters realized, because Nicholas had come to visit him in the very same hospital where his daughter was in Intensive Care, and had never said a word about it. Nicholas had talked about nothing but tennis, his new live-in love, and his work. Apparently he had never given Colleen a thought. The conversation had revolved around the cases he was handling, and how different and how much better than Emily Maureen Theiss was as a bed partner. He had mentioned in passing what Maureen's two children were doing, but not a word about his own daughter.

As Peters mulled over Nicholas's behavior, he reached for a pad and began to write down orders for his secretary to carry out in the morning. Nicholas, he thought with a satisfied smile, wasn't going to like this one bit.

Emily checked the log for the next round of medications and noticed that someone had forgotten to reorder Mrs. Cooper's new meds for arthritis. She had barely filled out the requisition and placed it in the slot where it would be picked up sometime during the next hour when Keith stopped by to talk.

"Ready for tomorrow?" he asked conspiratorially, though there wasn't another soul at the desk.

"What are you talking about?" Emily asked. She didn't look up from the notes that she was writing.

"The *Mercury*, Emily. I know Bill told you that tomorrow's lead story would be on Ridge."

Emily turned slowly to him. Somehow she had thought the story would be a long time in the writing. She had even thought that perhaps nothing would ever come of it, and Ridge's dirty secrets might be swept under the rug.

"Bill said that the first section is going to deal with the attitude of the hospital toward the poor and minorities, using John Alvarez as the prime example. The next segment will deal with what happens to members of the staff who don't knuckle under to the prevailing attitudes. That's where you come into it. Sounds like dynamite, doesn't it?''

"It sounds like we could all be out on the street collecting unemployment if your friend isn't careful!" Emily said tartly. She was already regretting her willingness to talk to Bill Sonderson. But damn it, O'Shea had almost managed to kill her daughter. He had to be called to task for that. But maybe she should have gone through regular channels, approached the problem from a different angle, one that didn't leave her quite so vulnerable.

Emily had met with Bill Sonderson during the time she had taken off. The newspaperman had come to her house, and they had spoken together for some time. He had been more than interested in her papers, and had talked to her about the episode, taping the entire conversation.

Sonderson had also been anxious to talk to Terry Barnall, but there had never been time, so he'd taken a short statement over the phone about Colleen's condition.

Bill Sonderson had finally decided to go with the data he had gathered from the other services. With the information he had picked up from Ob Gyn, Thoracic, and several other areas, he knew that the problem was prevalent and growing—people with real medical needs were systematically being shunted aside in favor of the rich, the influential, and the white.

"Don't worry about the hospital taking action against you. He's promised anonymity to everyone he's interviewed. Bill's a good guy. If they try anything, he'll see that every person in the Western Hemisphere knows about it. Ridge wouldn't dare risk that kind of adverse publicity.''

"Right," Emily said, but she knew better. Hospitals like Ridge could do anything they wanted, and fighting back was neither profitable or easy.

And yet, there had been a real change in the way Shelby and O'Shea had cared for John Alvarez after they realized who he was. John had been kept in Constant Care for days after he could have been moved back down to a regular floor. O'Shea had been hedging all his bets. Only last night, Emily had finally had a chance to invite Terry over for dinner, and they had talked about the newspaper story and its possible effect on Ridge. "I've done just about everything I can here to change the attitudes of people like O'Shea. Luckily, I don't have to stay here," Terry told her. "Two more weeks, and I'm gone. I'm finished at Ridge. I've got another place to go for research, and I'm signing the papers tomorrow afternoon." Emily's heart plummeted when she heard that he was leaving. She was very upset, but she hadn't said anything at all about it to Terry. They had spent the rest of the evening talking, and never once had she gathered up the courage to ask him what his plans were regarding her. She was terribly afraid that if she did, he would look startled or chagrined, and tell her that he had no plans at all involving her.

Now Emily poured Coralie's pills into a little plastic cup and headed down the corridor without another word to Keith.

Keith watched her go and shook his head. Emily was acting downright weird tonight. She should have been interested in the story that was coming out in the *Mercury*. She should have been asking all kinds of questions. Instead, she had just stopped talking to him and had gone back to filling medications. If he hadn't known how experienced and careful she was, he might have suggested that she watch what she was doing before she gave someone the wrong tablets. Something was bugging her, all right.

Silly, stupid woman, to think that a couple of meals and a few kisses meant anything to Terry. Think of it—building a whole romantic scenario on something as flimsy as that, Emily chided herself over and over. But the fact was, it hurt. She cared about him. She had really hoped for more. . . . Emily stopped in the middle of what she was doing, and her fingers touched her lips. The way they had kissed, she had hoped he might eventually fall in love with her.

She carried the little cup of pills into Coralie's room.

"Stupid!" she said aloud, chastising herself.

"Who are you calling stupid, missy?" Coralie demanded.

"Oh, Coralie!" Emily blushed. "I'd never say such a thing to you. I was saying it to myself," she told the old woman.

"Good, because I may be old and I may be frail, but I'm *not* stupid. And one thing I can see for sure is that you're pining for a young man. Does he know it?"

Emily stared at Coralie, not believing her ears. How on earth could she know such a thing?

Coralie chuckled. "I told you I wasn't stupid. Look at you, standing there in a fog, dreaming about him. What's wrong? Why aren't you managing to make a go of the romance?"

Emily laughed, a short, bitter sound. "There *isn't* a romance."

"Here—stick out your palm and let me see." Coralie grabbed Emily's hand and turned it so she could see the palm.

189

Emily felt the grip slacken slightly, and she tried to wrest her hand away. That was the hand with all the scars, the hand she never showed anyone if she could help it.

"Hush now, girl—I've seen hands much worse than this, and they don't bother me a bit," Coralie said as she peered at the long, white scars that disfigured the palm of Emily's hand.

"Please . . . I have patients to see," Emily said, not knowing just how to handle this. She could have broken the contact easily, but she was so afraid of damaging Coralie's only good hand that she restrained the impulse to pull away.

"You've been through some tragedy. I see here that there was a death with your first love. Was that in the fire?"

Emily stared at the old woman, wondering just what she'd gotten herself into. Was Coralie really psychic? She might guess about the fire from the scars, but there was no way she could have known that Emily's husband had died in the same fire.

"It . . . was," she finally managed to say.

"Shame you didn't have any children with him. You should have. But, ah—what's this? A big mistake, a *terrible* mistake, with the second man in your life."

"I notice you didn't call him my second love," Emily said dryly.

"More like the big *hate* of your life. And he probably deserves it," Coralie said serenely. "Now stop that squirming, girl, and let me get on with this. Most people beg to have me do this, but I don't very often now that I'm old." Coralie's grip was stronger than Emily would have thought possible for a hand ravaged by arthritis. Coralie continued, "But I did earn a packet of money a good many years back. We never went hungry in the Depression, let me tell you! There were always plenty of people who wanted to know what was coming, if they were sure that the person doing the telling would give them the straight skinny. Only started one fight, too, in all that time. That was when I told a man he'd better be looking for another woman because the one he was with wasn't the most trustworthy kind. Silly man wasn't using the eyes God gave him. His girl was out there where I could see her, flirting with anything that had button trousers on. She wasn't the girl for a man like him, and I let him know it. Oh, he was mad! Took a swing at me and then started in on the tent.

"Well, when he started the fight, I yelled for help using the old carnie signal of 'Hey, Rube,' and before you know it, the whole place was up in arms. We were told to leave town that very night. I don't believe the circus ever went back there," Coralie said.

All the time she had been talking, she had been looking down at Emily's hand, following the lines. She didn't use just the palms. She got her best impressions when she was listening to what a person's skin and blood and thoughts told her. There were a lot of other things that helped her be so accurate, though she'd never have told her secrets to anyone for anything in the world.

"There's a big change coming. It's both terrible and wonderful. It's love, loss, and everything that tragedies and celebrations are made of," she said now.

"Coralie, you'd better tell me more than that!"

"It's love of the kind you want. But I can't tell more because I can't see it in your palm. You'll know soon enough. Just don't despair. Your child will be all right," Coralie said, then she released Emily, rubbing her hand over her eyes. "Now, be off with you. I have to go to sleep. For shame, keeping an old woman like me up so long! Don't you know I'm supposed to get my beauty rest? I'm going to a nursing home tomorrow, Dr. Mendelsohn says. And then in a month or so, I'll be back home, with a restraining order on that punk grandson of mine. He won't ever have a chance to do something like that to an old woman again." Coralie sounded determined, but Emily could see the deep sadness in the old woman's heart as she spoke about her only living kin.

As Emily left the room, she wondered if Coralie had been able to foresee the tragedy in her own life.

Chapter Fourteen

"Hey, Emily, time to wake up, sleepyhead!"

Nora knocked briskly on the door, rousing Emily from a sound sleep.

Emily moaned and turned over. She had had a terrible time trying to get to sleep. First she had worried about what could be done about her romance with Terry—at least it was a romance on her end, but she wasn't certain that it was on his. And then there had been the call from Bill Sonderson. She had been so shocked by his unexpected news that by the time she finally calmed down enough to fall asleep, she was hours behind schedule and exhausted.

Emily looked at the clock. It was almost eight P.M. That meant she had already missed putting Colleen to bed—Nora would have taken care of that when she came home from the office.

Both Nora and Emily had been watching only
like a pair of hawks, making sure they probably
getting enough rest, eating properly, and help it. Col-
if there wasn't a chill in the air. They to believe she
overprotecting her, but Emily and to believe she
leen had been so sick that hospital, stayed home a
had been released from right back to school. From
couple of days, and go one would have ever known
the way she behaved died.
that she had al

It had been a remarkable recovery, even Terry
Purnall had said so. So far there had been no signs of
residual damage. Colleen could hear and see perfectly well, she was bright as a button, and she had more
energy than her mother would ever have thought
possible.

Emily wished she had the same kind of energy.
Right now, she didn't want to get up. She just wanted
to stay in bed and think about her problems until she
found simple, easy answers to everything that was
bothering her.

The first problem she had worried over during the
morning was her relationship with Terry. What could
she possibly do about him? She found him extremely
attractive, and something about Terry had touched a
need she hadn't even realized existed. But it was
obvious that Terry didn't feel the same way about her.
She had finally decided that the only conclusion
possible was to accept what he was willing to give
her. If he regarded her only as a friend, there was
nothing she could do to change his perception. In
spite of his declaration that he'd like to go out with
her, he hadn't done anything about it.

Emily had thought about it while she drove Colleen
to school and was still thinking about it when she
decided that she wasn't going to manage a morning

nap. Instead, she had sat at the sewing machine and started making a new skirt for Colleen. While she sewed she wondered what sort of woman would appeal to a man like Terry. What was it about her that hadn't held his interest?

She turned a seam and sewed it, racing blindly along, thinking about his kiss.

"Ridiculous," she told herself, "pining like this for a man you've only kissed a few times. Act your age."

But Emily hadn't found that acting thirty was a whole lot different than acting twenty. The problem could still be stated in one word—men.

"It happens," Emily had finally told herself sadly. "People think they'd be great together, and then they find out that that magic isn't there for one of them. The sparks just don't fly. Nothing to fret about, is it?"

The words were right, she finally concluded, but the message wasn't getting through to her brain. She had allowed herself to think about a future with Terry, but she had been so hungry for the kindness he had shown that she had probably misread his intentions all along. He had come over to eat, not to propose marriage. He had been a good, kind, efficient doctor when Colleen was so sick. That didn't automatically mean that he saw Colleen as a possible stepdaughter, or Emily as the kind of woman he could become involved with. He had kissed her, and it had been warm and tender and gentle. For Emily, there had been sparks that had warmed her in ways she had almost forgotten. Maybe it hadn't done anything for Terry except to serve as a pleasant moment of flesh against flesh. She had built too much on it, and now she was going to have to live with the fact that he was leaving the hospital and she was being left behind.

When Emily finally managed to stop the merry-go-round of wishes and push the thoughts about Terry out of her mind, the ongoing worry about the bills invaded. They hadn't gone away, more was the pity. The bills were still there, waiting to be paid. She had almost caught up with the power bill, and she had another check coming in within the next few days. But every time Emily looked at what remained unpaid, it made her want to cry. How was she ever going to get ahead if there was more money going out than there was coming in?

"Damn Leopold Peters anyway!" Emily swore. She was so tired of trying to treat him like any other patient when the man really should have been placed on a rack and pulled limb from limb. And under other circumstances, she'd be the one to do it!

The phone rang, finally distracting her mind from both Peters and the bills.

"Mrs. Greer? This is Bill Sonderson. I just wanted to let you know that the first article should be in either the late edition today, or the early edition tomorrow, depending on what's popping around the world. It looks like a dynamite series, and part of it is due to your willingness to talk to us."

Emily thanked him. It was kind of him to tell her that she had been useful, but she sensed that there was another reason for his call.

"By the way, has anyone from the hospital called you this morning?" Sonderson asked.

"No—why? I'm not on duty and evidently no one needed extra help, because I wasn't called for overtime."

"Look, I hate to just leap in with this news, but I need to know—did Dr. O'Shea have a drinking problem, something that was generally known 'round the hospital?"

'ily frowned. "I don't think it was generally

196

known. The first time I thought there might be a problem was that night in the Emergency Room. Why do you ask?"

There was a brief silence, and then Bill answered, "Because O'Shea was in a smash-up this morning. Three cars involved, one fatality, and it looks like O'Shea might not make it. He's at Ridge in critical condition at the moment."

Emily sat down quickly. She could barely breathe, the shock was so great. Yet she couldn't help feeling that the man deserved it. She tried to ignore her flicker of elation, but remembered that she had wished it on him when he hurt Colleen.

"What happened?" she finally managed to regain her voice enough to ask.

"He was driving home after finishing up at the hospital, we think—it was on the route from the hospital to his house, at least. Seems he had been nipping at a bottle somewhere along the way. He had a blood-alcohol level of point one-nine percent, almost twice the legal limit for a drunk-driving arrest."

Emily nodded. "I can't say I'm surprised. But what actually happened? How did the accident take place?"

"We're not completely certain, but an eyewitness said that O'Shea's Mercedes suddenly swerved toward an off ramp. Evidently he didn't look before he turned the wheel and rammed straight into the side of a big double semitractor-trailer. The Mercedes bounced back after the impact and headed across the road into the other two cars that had been traveling almost abreast of him. The driver of the yellow Camaro was killed when he hit the median strip and flipped, the other car was just dented, nothing serious, and the Mercedes was totaled. The only reason O'Shea didn't die was that his car was so heavy and so well built that it took the impact and wasn't completely crushed. The truck driver called for help on his C.B. If it hadn't been for him, O'Shea would probably have died waiting for an ambulance."

"Oh, Lord," Emily said. "That will certainly make an interesting tie-in with the series you're doing, won't it?"

"It won't hurt. The main thrust of the stories concerns the treatment received from some doctors, but it is mentioned in passing that part of the trouble could be from the high incidence of drug and alcohol use among health-care professionals. It may not always cause them to lose control, but certainly drugs and alcohol can impair someone's objectivity when assessing a medical crisis—as it did in Colleen's case, as a matter of fact."

"Thank you for calling. I'll check on Dr. O'Shea when I get in. Actually, I probably won't have to check anything—the major part of any conversation in Ridge tonight is bound to be about O'Shea. He wasn't well liked despite the fact that he was brilliant —or maybe it was *because* he was brilliant, and let all of us lesser lights know how dim we were compared to him."

"Do me a favor then, would you?" Bill Sonderson asked.

"Sure, if I can," Emily said cautiously.

"If you hear anything that we could find corroboration for regarding O'Shea and his drinking, let me know. It may not be printed, but it would be interesting to have on hand."

"I'll call," Emily promised.

They chatted for a few more moments, and then hung up.

So O'Shea was in Intensive Care. She should have felt compassion for him. It was a shock to Emily that she felt no sense of pity for the man at all. In fact, when she actually thought about it, she had to admit that she hated him with a depth and breadth that she wouldn't have believed possible.

"I didn't know I had it in me," Emily breathed. She realized that what she felt for Nicholas was only a pale shadow of what she experienced when she thought about O'Shea. Nicholas was an irritant, a man chiefly guilty of greed and selfishness. Now she knew that she only disliked him. Milton O'Shea had taught her what hatred was all about. . . .

Nora banged on the door again.

"Emily, will you please hustle your butt and get out here? I've been restraining myself from opening this huge envelope from Mr. Leopold Peters, but I can't wait much longer. The curiosity is killing me."

Emily's eyes flew open. An envelope from Peters? She certainly wasn't expecting anything, since he was still in the hospital.

She grabbed her soft blue robe and flung the door open, almost colliding with Nora.

"It's about time!" Nora said, forcing her back into the bedroom. "Rip it open before I do."

She handed Emily the envelope and waited, her hands on her hips, while Emily fumbled with the thick padding and reached into the package, scraping her hand on the staples that had held it closed. She pulled out the bulky papers that were inside.

"I don't believe it!" Emily gasped, her eyes widening as she stared at the check that had been paper-clipped to the letter on top of everything else.

There it was—a real, crackling-new, beautifully printed beige check from the firm of Peters, Greer, and Hamlin, in the amount of $253,044.21.

"Look at this," Emily breathed. "What do you think it is, a joke? Do you think he took everything out of the account and closed it and then sent me this check so I could watch it bounce?"

"What does the letter say?" Nora asked.

Emily skimmed the paper. "Payment in full for back child support, for alimony, for the balance due on the house, and for my share of the retirement fund! Peters says he had Nicholas sell some of the stocks and bonds that remained in his possession to get the cash over to us as soon as possible. And listen . . . " Emily read from the letter, " 'Please be assured that any remaining money due you for your daughter's care and for your own alimony for the three years agreed upon will be sent in timely fashion. My best to your daughter.' "

"Leopold Peters wrote that?" Nora asked incredulously. "I thought he came into the hospital for a hip replacement, not a *heart* replacement!"

Emily now opened the other papers that had been sent with the check. The thick blue folder contained the hotly contested deed to the house. Among the other bundles were a copy of the retirement-fund ledger, to assure her that she had actually received half the sum that had been deposited during the time she and Nicholas had been married, and an accounting sheet showing how her alimony and child-care payments had been made. There was also a folder showing that Colleen was still being carried on Nicholas's health insurance and would continue to be until she was eighteen, or twenty-one if she chose to go to college. It was all there!

Emily sat on the edge of the bed holding the check and wept tears of relief. It was finally over. She was free now to do whatever she wanted. Whatever she decided, it would no longer be tainted with daily battles with Nicholas over the money he owed her and Colleen.

"So, what are you going to do with it all?" Nora asked, echoing Emily's thoughts.

"First, I'm going down to the bank first thing tomorrow morning when I come off duty and deposit the check. I'll have the bank certify that there are enough funds in Peters's account to cover it. Once the money has really been posted to my account and paid by Peters's bank, I'm going to pay off every single bill, and then I'm going out to buy a new pair of shoes!" Emily looked over at the old white oxfords she had been wearing for months, despite the fact that they were raggedy and worn down and made her feet ache every night she was on duty.

"Wonderful," Nora said dryly. "You're holding a check for over two hundred thousand dollars, and you're thinking about your *feet*?"

"First things first."

"What about quitting your job at Ridge? After what you've just gone through, I'd sure as hell be thinking about it," Nora said.

"Actually, ever since I saw that check, I've been thinking about the life Nicholas and I led—you know, the prominent attorney and his charming, decorative wife. Well, that didn't work out too well for either of us. I don't do decoration well, and all Nicholas really cared about was making money. Which, as is obvious from the total settlement, he did rather well. But it was never enough for him, and it certainly wasn't good for me."

"What are you getting at?" Nora asked.

"I've been thinking about my life and what I really want to do. Since it looks like I'm not going to have my first choice, I think I'll consider the alternatives," Emily mused.

"What would first choice be?"

Emily thought for a moment. She didn't usually

open up easily and confide in anyone, not even Nora. She had never talked to Nora about Terry, except to say that she was much obliged for the way he had taken over and helped Colleen.

"Come on, what are you afraid of—that I'll announce it to the world?" Nora asked.

"No. It's just that it doesn't have a snowball's chance in hell of coming true. I wish it did, but . . ."

"Come on," Nora said impatiently.

"I wish I had a chance to get married to a guy I really like, and settle down. I'd keep on being a nurse, of course, but it sure would be nice . . ."

"Is there anyone particular in this rosy picture, or are we talking about a generic Mr. Nice?"

"Terry Barnall," Emily finally admitted.

Nora looked at her and whistled. "Well, when you decide you want a romance, you do it up right! Are you sure it isn't a case of hero worship because he saved Colleen's life? It's been known to happen, you know. I've heard all the stories about doctors being pestered by women who thought they'd fallen in love with them after having been through a health crisis."

Emily shot her a scornful look. "For pete's sake, Nora, you should know better than that! Most of the time I don't even *like* doctors. I certainly don't worship them—and besides, this started before Colleen got meningitis, not after."

Nora raised her hands, playfully warding off Emily's anger. "Okay, I get the point. Then I suppose you'd be interested in a message from Terry Barnall?"

"I'd be very interested," Emily said. At least she would be, as long as it wasn't a message saying that Terry had called to say good-bye.

"He called around three-thirty this afternoon. You

were sound asleep, and he said not to disturb you. But he'd like to make a date with you for the morning, after your shift. Something about going out for breakfast to a little candlelit restaurant."

Emily's heart took a crazy spin. Hope flooded through her, lifting her spirits. Maybe things would work out after all!

"I'll leave a message for him . . . oh, damn, I can't! I have to come right home and take Colleen to school . . ." She looked hopefully at Nora.

"Nope—I'm sorry, but even in the interest of true love I can't be late tomorrow morning. I've got a brief to get out, and it's going to take every minute I have tomorrow to finish it up on time."

Emily thought for a moment and then brightened.

"How about a small, intimate candlelit breakfast here? I mean, we'd have the whole house to ourselves after I take Colleen to school . . ." She stopped and blushed. It sounded like she was actually setting up a seduction!

"Sounds fine. Come on, I'll help you. You've got at least an hour and a half until you have to head down to the hospital. In that time we should be able to get everything ready. Want me to start by taking some of the cinnamon rolls out of the freezer?"

It actually took less than twenty minutes to make orange juice, put the rolls out, and set the table with Emily's best linen and silver. She realized she was taking an awful chance, building up her hopes like this. Terry might just want to take her out to breakfast to tell her that he was leaving in the next week and to tell her he'd enjoyed knowing her. In fact, she thought glumly, that was probably exactly what was going to happen. She looked at the table, surveying the tablecloth, the silver and china, and the candles.

It was too much. She wouldn't ever be able to look at a fancy table again if he told her he was leaving, and thank you very much for the friendship.

She put away the silver and china, folded the linen tablecloth, and replaced it with a plain blue covering and the everyday blue crockery that she, Nora, and Colleen always used. It wasn't as fancy, but at least she wouldn't have made a fool of herself if Terry just wanted to let her down gently.

"There, that looks better," she decided, satisfied. Not too formal—not as if she anticipated a proposal of marriage, or a declaration of undying love. Just a nice place for two friends to have breakfast and talk about what each of them would be doing in the next few weeks.

Still, she wished she could have gone out to breakfast with Terry.

"Better he realizes what it's like when there's a child to be taken care of first. Of course he already knows that—maybe that's why he decided to back off."

Emily was very much afraid that might be the answer. He knew by now that her first priority would always be Colleen.

There wasn't time for more speculation. She had to hurry to make her shift at Ridge.

Chapter Fifteen

"Emily, wait a second!" Keith called. He had seen her walking toward the hospital, and ran to catch up with her.

"Hi, Keith, what's the hurry?" Emily said.

"I need to talk to you. First of all, I wanted to say that it's been nice working with you. I've enjoyed the rapport we've had on the floor."

"What do you mean, 'it's been nice working with you?' You're not leaving Ridge, are you?" Emily stopped in the middle of the street, then had to run a few quick steps to get out of the way of a car that had no intention of stopping.

"Not after Bill's articles, I won't be," Keith said calmly. "I saw what he wrote—he brought it over for me to look at, to make certain that he wasn't scuttling anyone. I told him I didn't care if he used my name, and he did."

"Oh, Keith, why did you let him do it? It isn't fair

that you're going to end up without a job. What will you do?" Emily couldn't help thinking about the kind of position she'd be in if she were fired. "Besides, maybe you're anticipating trouble. I can't see how the hospital would be able to do anything at all about your talking to the newspapers. The nursing administration would probably be on your side," Emily said. "We've all had trouble with discrimination. It isn't always as blatant as the kind of trouble you had with Shelby, but we women are often on the receiving end of the kind of sexist attitudes that have caused trouble for you."

"I don't mind the sexism. I don't even mind being called the 'spade nurse' behind my back—no one has ever had the nerve to say it to my face!" Keith flexed his muscles. The seams on his white shirt strained under the pressure. For a moment, he looked every bit the wrestler he had once been.

Emily suppressed a smile. She wouldn't want to call Keith names where he could hear it, either. He looked far too formidable.

"However," Keith continued after he relaxed and assumed his normal slightly slouching posture again, "I *do* mind having my ability as a nurse questioned, and that's happened in every conversation I've had with Dr. Shelby for the last six months."

"But you're going to lose your job because of Shelby. Don't be silly! Residents come and go, but nurses are forever," Emily said. She'd often told herself the same thing when faced with a particularly difficult medical student.

"Normally I wouldn't have thought about it, but put it all together and it makes sense. This story is going to make me a real target. John went home a couple of days ago, and he's fully recovered, so I don't have to fight to keep him alive—he can take care of himself. Then there's Shelby's attitude and the way I'm beginning to feel about Ridge itself, as a corporation and a hospital. Well, that offer of a job from the neuro rehabilitation facility looks better all the time. Besides, they've upped the offer to thirty-seven thousand dollars a year. I think I'm going to be their star performer. I'm male and I'm black, and that should satisfy two of their equal-opportunity-program objectives at one time. And I'd like to work with head-trauma patients who have a chance to improve. It beats working with patients who are going to die!''

Emily was silent for a moment. She could hear so many things in Keith's words, problems that were mirrored in her own life. She'd dealt with them in her own way; now Keith was having to make choices, and the idea of moving on wasn't a bad decision.

"When do you expect to turn in your resignation?"

"Tonight. I'll hand it to Denise and forward a copy to Administration tomorrow morning. I should be out of here by the end of April."

"I wish you luck. Sometime soon I'm going to have to sit down and think about my options, too," Emily said as they entered the hospital.

She stopped by one of the in-house phones and placed a call to Terry Barnall. Within a very short time, she had been patched through to him. She couldn't believe her luck. It was almost a certainty that no matter when someone called the neurosurgical residents, they were always busy.

"Yeah, give me a second, will you?" She could hear Terry yelling at whoever was calling him. "Terry Barnall here—can I help you?"

"Hi, Terry, this is Emily. My housemate said you'd called?"

"I want to get together with you in the morning. I

have a promise, in writing, that short of a national catastrophe, I'll be able to take a whole hour and a half off. I need to talk to you," Terry said.

Emily listened to his voice and wondered if she were misreading it. He sounded happy, like he was smiling while he talked to her. Of course it could have been just because he was glad at the way his career was going and he wanted to talk to her about it, but still . . . there was the possibility that he was just happy to hear her voice.

"Sounds fine," Emily said.

"Good. There's a Magic Pan down the street that's doing a special early-bird breakfast. They've got the best seafood crêpe known to man. How does that sound?"

Emily crossed her fingers as well as she could while holding the phone. Here goes, she said to herself. Here's where he finds out what it's really like to make a date with a single mother.

"Terry, I can't," Emily finally managed to say.

There was a silence on the other end of the line.

"I'm sorry, Emily, I thought . . . well, I guess I just assumed that . . . hell!" Terry stopped abruptly, the expletive echoing in the air.

Emily thrilled just a little bit. Didn't it sound almost as if he had hoped they could be together, because he enjoyed being with her?

"Please don't be angry. It's just that I have to go straight home, make certain that Colleen is up and ready to go to school. And since Nora has to be at the office on time with no delays, I have to drive Colleen to school," Emily explained.

"Oh, is *that* all!" Terry's voice didn't sound nearly so tight. There was some shouting in the background, and whoever it was sounded irritated. "Yeah, just a second," Terry yelled back.

"I know you're in a hurry, and I also know it isn't The Magic Pan, but how about something to eat at my house, after I get Colleen ready and off to school?" Emily asked.

"That's even better. I'd like to talk to you in private, anyway," Terry said. His voice sounded happy again.

"I'm off at seven. Want to meet me in the lobby?"

"Fine. See you then, Emily. Damn it, I'm *coming*!" Terry roared, and severed the connection.

Emily was glad there were some interesting new patients on the floor. She needed eight hours' worth of distractions to carry her through until she met Terry.

"Emily, can you step over here for a second?" Denise called. "I hate to do this, but Angela just called in. She's got the flu, and can't even get out of bed. We're going to have to split her load. I've called the agency and they can't send out anyone for this shift, so it's up to us."

"That's fine," Emily said, taking the two charts that Denise handed her.

"Keith, here are your extra two." Denise gave him the metal folders.

Keith started to frown and then let out a startled whoop as he caught sight of the name. It was totally unprofessional, unexpected, and delightful.

"What's up?" Denise was frowning at him.

"Look who you gave me! I've got to get down there and see her . . . she *lived*, damn it! She pulled through!"

Keith didn't stop to explain as he ran down the hallway and stopped at the doorway, peering in almost as if he couldn't believe his eyes.

"Hey, Keith! I asked them to put you on my case tonight, if you were on. I'm glad Denise did." Cynda Arden was propped up in bed, looking better than she had in weeks. Her awful pallor had retreated, and she was breathing easier than she had since she checked into the hospital. She took another few stitches in the new quilt she was working on, and pulled the thread through, smiling at him.

"Cynda, what happened?" Keith was positively glowing, he was so glad to see the girl. Cynda had been one of the main reasons he had decided to move over to the neuro rehabilitation facility. He'd seen death many times before, but this particular patient had touched him deeply. He had finally decided that he'd seen enough. He couldn't stand another Cynda. Every day when he'd called up to the ICU, he'd expected to be told she had died. He hadn't even bothered to call the last two nights—he'd been too depressed at the thought of having his worst fears confirmed.

And here she was, almost the picture of health.

"Tell me what happened," he repeated. He had her chart in his hand—he could have found out from that, but it would be more fun to hear it from her own lips.

"A miracle, maybe," Cynda said. "There's a doctor here doing some experimental work with a new antibiotic. That combined with a new therapy he's working on to keep the damage to a minimum, and we won this one. Not only that, but it looks like my chronic pneumonia that's been a problem for so many years may be helped by the antibiotic. I might even live to see those nieces of mine start off to school! It's like a great, glorious gift, and I'm going to use every second I have. Because for a while there, Keith, the angel of death was sitting right there by my shoulder, waiting for me." For a moment Cynda looked very somber.

Then she caught sight of an envelope sitting on her

bedside stand. "Hey, I almost forgot! Look—I got a letter from Lara Mendoza this morning, just as I was being transferred back down here. She says that she's trying something new. She's had her husband dismiss the servants and she's actually beginning to learn how to keep house."

Cynda took the letter out of the envelope and opened it. The fragrance from the paper was as exotic as Lara herself. "'I'm changing my life a little. Perhaps you might be right. Maybe I do need to leave a memory of me as something other than an invalid. I'm not sure you are totally right, but I'm convinced enough to try and make a change.'"

"What do you think of that?" Cynda was beaming as she stuck the letter back in the envelope.

"I think you're wonderful." Keith grinned at her and then couldn't restrain himself. He reached over and gave her a big hug.

"Mr. Jennings, you will come here this instant!" Dr. Shelby's voice cut through the scene.

Cynda patted Keith on the back.

"Better go see what she wants. I know I should be grateful to her—she's one of my doctors—but she has the bedside manner of a shark!" Cynda whispered to him.

Keith smothered a laugh. Cynda had the woman pegged perfectly. Then he went out into the hallway to confront Dr. Shelby.

"Keith Jennings, would you care to explain your conduct?" Shelby was glaring at him, her face red with anger.

"My conduct?" Keith said blankly. He didn't have any idea what the woman was going on about now. She seemed to take a perverse pleasure in picking on everything he did—the way he looked at her, his question about a medication, or almost anything else.

"Mr. Jennings, are you going to tell me that I didn't see what you just did?"

"What I just did?" Keith repeated. He'd only been here ten minutes—what could he have done in that time?

"Don't play games with me! I warned you about your behavior many times before, and now you have just given me grounds to report you to the nursing administration and to insist that you be dismissed!"

Keith had had enough. He couldn't stand the sight of her, the sound of her, or one more minute of her ranting.

"What the hell are you talking about, woman?" he roared.

"Keith, please . . ." Denise Frazier had heard the rumble of trouble down the hallway and had come over to see what was happening. From the looks of it, she had intervened just in time.

"No, Denise, let's hear what this miserable specimen of coprolite has to say," Keith said.

"*Coprolite*?" Dr. Shelby repeated. She was wide-eyed and had assumed her usual defensive posture.

"Coprolite—fossilized feces!" Keith snarled.

Dr. Shelby looked stunned and then she started to scream at Keith. "Don't you insult me! Don't you *dare* say such a thing to me! Are you calling me *shit*? Is that what you said?"

"If it fits," Keith said tightly.

"I'll report you for this, as well as for going in there and fondling that young girl! Imagine what her parents would say—imagine what *anyone* would say—if they knew that we had a male nurse, a *black* male nurse at that, who touched female patients! We'd be sued in an instant for sexual abuse!" Shelby was screaming now. She had finally snapped. She was going to tell him just what she thought about scum

212

like him. Keith Jennings should never have been allowed in nursing school! Ridge should never have hired him!

"Keith, did you touch a patient in an unprofessional manner?" Denise asked calmly.

"I did not." Keith drew himself up to his full height, and was facing Dr. Shelby, gradually edging her closer and closer to the wall.

"He *did*! I saw him! He went into that room right there, and he actually put his arms around that little girl with cystic fibrosis. Cynda's one of my patients, and I *know* she would never have allowed it if she hadn't been frightened by his physical size, and probably by his color!" Shelby insisted.

"Dr. Shelby, that is quite enough," Denise said.

"But he *did*, I tell you! He did! I saw him. He can't lie about it, I *saw* him!" Shelby was almost in tears now. Her face was flushed, and she looked as if at any minute she was going to start foaming at the mouth.

"He did put his arms around me," Cynda intervened. Her voice was quiet but it cut through Shelby's hysterics.

"Cynda . . . what are you doing out of bed?" Keith asked, and rushed to her side. She looked wobbly, and it was obvious that she was using the IV pole for support. She had thrown her robe over her shoulders since she couldn't actually put it on with the IV in place. She shivered as she stood there.

"Cynda, don't worry about this. Just get back to bed. You'll get sick again, and then you'll be back up there with pneumonia." Keith was really worried about the girl.

"What I'm doing, Keith, is defending my friend against a woman who should never have been allowed near anyone in the human race, much less around patients who need and expect emotional and physical support from their doctor," Cynda stated. "You're a kind, caring human being, Keith, not like *her*!"

Shelby turned on her. "What do you mean? I've always been good to you!"

"No, you haven't been good to me. You've turned your back on me when I needed help, because I'm a CF patient. The fact that I was going to die soon made it all right for you to ignore me. And when you weren't ignoring me, you were refusing to take care of other patients who needed your help. One of those patients was Mexican so that was all right, too! You and Dr. O'Shea thought you could run your department any way you wanted and no one would be the wiser. Well, you were wrong! If anyone should be kicked out of Ridge, it's you!"

"Cynda, this is too much for you. Please let me take you back to bed," Keith asked. He put his arm around her and tried to turn her back to the room.

"See? There—he's doing it again! He's touching her. *Fire him*, I'm telling you, fire him! Fire him before he rapes her. Fire him before he goes berserk!"

"I'm going to call security!" Denise grabbed Emily's arm as she hurried by, trying to ignore the commotion, though she'd heard every word that had been said. "We've got a problem on our hands."

Emily glanced over at Shelby.

"Dr. Shelby, come with me," Emily said, stepping between the doctor and Keith.

"No, no, leave me alone!" Shelby screamed.

"Right now, this instant. Come with me to the nurses' lounge." Emily's tone was calm, authoritative.

Surprisingly, Shelby allowed Emily to pull her

away from Keith and Denise. A few more steps, and they were in the nurses' lounge.

"Sit down, Dr. Shelby," Emily ordered.

"My name is . . . Rachel," Shelby answered, still on the thin edge of hysteria.

"Okay, Rachel. What happened? I'm surprised no one noticed that you smell like a bourbon factory, and you can't even hold your hands still. How much did you drink before you came up and confronted Keith?"

Shelby hiccuped.

"I don't know—a few drinks. Not much. It was . . .", she paused for a moment, then tried again. "It was—in memoriam. Dr. O'Shea died this afternoon at four-thirty-one. I was there when it happened. . . ."

Emily felt the shock race through her. Yes, she had wished him dead, but then it hadn't been real. Now it was, and she wished she had never harbored such a thought.

"I'm sorry," Emily said quietly.

"No, you aren't, and neither is anyone else. He was drinking too much and he was making awful mistakes—like he did with your daughter. I knew what was going on, but I wasn't going to say anything. . . ."

"Why not?" Emily asked. Better to let her pour it all out right now, than let it fester and burst forth in another bout of craziness. The administration took a dim view of their residents hurling insults at the nurses, particularly when that nurse was male and black. "Why didn't you do anything about it?"

"Because I knew that if I didn't play along with him, I'd never get another chance at a residency. My grades are fine, I have everything going for me there, but I have no feel for the patients. I just can't get involved with them, and so I make mistakes. You have to be able to see the patients as human beings, and I don't. They're not people I know, they're mostly not from my social class. They're nothing to me. . . ."

Shelby was looking at Emily, pleading for understanding.

Emily was sorry for the woman, but she didn't understand. She said, "Then, Dr. Shelby, if you manage to survive this mess, I suggest that you think about going into research. Because there isn't a hospital in the world that would knowingly accept a physician with your limitations."

"I know. That's why I grabbed the opportunity to be with Milton—Dr. O'Shea. We went to bed, we drank together, we were *important* to each other. He put up with the way I was, because he was that way, too. He's practically the only person in my whole life who liked me."

It was a pathetic confession. Emily, however, was not moved.

"Instead of telling you how wonderful you were, someone should have taught you manners a long time ago. Who ever told you that having a temper tantrum because a nurse is happy to see a patient, and the patient is happy to see him, was an acceptable reaction on your part? Didn't it even occur to you that this was none of your business?"

"I thought he was intimidating her. . . ."

"You did not. You saw it as a God-given chance to go after Keith again. You didn't expect it to turn into a full-fledged confrontation, did you?"

"It was *wrong*, do you hear me, wrong! He *forced* her to say it was all right!"

"He didn't pull her out of bed and drag her out into the hallway to tell you that Keith was her friend and you had repeatedly acted like the spoiled, insecure little girl you are." Emily didn't pull any punches.

"I'll have you fired for that," Shelby said fiercely.

"No, I don't think you will, Rachel. First of all, think what this incident is going to look like on your record. Someone is going to write you up, because you simply cannot go around spouting racial slurs and expect it to be overlooked. Do you really want to make things even worse for yourself by complaining to Nursing Administration about me?"

Shelby looked at Emily and then slowly shook her head. She was almost back to normal now. Her terrible rage had subsided, and she had stopped sniffling. The enormity of what she had done was beginning to hit her as the effect of the alcohol she had consumed was dissipated.

"What should I do?" she quavered.

Almost as an answer to her, a female security guard came into the room and motioned for Shelby to come with her, saying, "There are a couple of people who would like to talk to you downstairs. Please bring your belongings with you." She didn't smile at Shelby as she led her away.

Emily was left alone for a few minutes in the nurses' lounge. She hadn't even begun looking after her patients, and already she was frazzled. It was going to be a long night.

Chapter Sixteen

Denise put her head in her hands. She felt as if she'd been through a wringer. This was the last straw, the worst of the nightmares that could happen to her. She'd apologized to Keith and assured him that nothing Dr. Shelby had said would ever see the light of day. She'd had to ask if he wanted to file a grievance with the nurses' union, because he was certainly entitled to have his case heard. Denise had never come up against such blatant discrimination in all her life, and of course it had happened on *her* shift! She still couldn't believe that Dr. Shelby had actually stood there and said such things, as if every word were both acceptable and logical.

Denise Frazier had been a nurse for almost ten years, and in that time she had seen her share of residents come and go. During that time she'd seen a couple who she thought should never have been allowed in medical school. But she had never before been faced with a resident who chose to have a nervous breakdown. And if that wasn't bad enough, there was the newspaper lying on her desk. She looked down at the *Mercury* again and trembled as she scanned the headline:

"RIDGE CRISIS—WHO LIVES AND WHO DIES.

Access to the finest medical care in the city may be systematically denied to minorities and to the poor at the city's largest and best-equipped hospital."

The story went on to give a background of Ridge's history, and then proceeded to discuss a case of discrimination that had happened on Ridge Six East.

"John Alvarez was dying of a bullet wound to the chest. Trauma and infection had caused massive damage to his lungs. Mr. Alvarez was originally placed in the hospital's Constant Care Unit, where he could be monitored closely for any change in his condition. Within twenty-four hours of his admission, at a time when the need for care was critical, John Alvarez was transferred out of Constant Care to Ridge Six East. Why was he transferred? Because another patient who was white, rich, and socially prominent was admitted to the hospital with a minor chest contusion and allegedly required Mr. Alvarez's bed.

"It was only through the quick action of two nurses on Ridge Six East that John Alvarez is alive today. Keith Jennings and Denise Frazier refused to accept the patient transfer, insisting on another evaluation by the resident who had ordered the change from Constant Care to a general floor. Through their efforts, Dr.

Rachel Shelby, the chief resident in thoracic surgery, was forced to acknowledge her error, and John Alvarez was returned to Constant Care. John Alvarez is alive and well today, but if Ridge's apparent policy of giving preferential treatment to the white and wealthy had not been challenged, the First National Trustee Bank would have lost one of their chief operating officers."

The story continued on another page, but Denise couldn't bring herself to follow it to the bitter end.

She had been named. It didn't matter whether the mention was laudatory or otherwise—Ridge didn't like being in the news.

As a result, tonight's episode was bound to come out. Denise would be questioned, and so would Keith. Nursing Administration might be delighted that they had stood up to the doctor and insisted on proper care for John Alvarez, but the general administration of the hospital wouldn't see it that way. They were reactionary, old-line doctors, and they would make Denise's life miserable for having openly questioned one of their own. Worse, they were going to realize that not only had she questioned Shelby, but she had forced the doctor to give in to her demands.

Denise finally flipped the page. Her eyes followed the line of print to the last paragraph, set in bold type.

"Tomorrow—What happens to a nurse at Ridge who refuses to accept blame for a patient's self-destructive conduct?"

That had to be Emily Greer. How was Denise ever going to explain why their floor, their section, had been mentioned by name in this exposé? Heads were going to roll left and right. Denise knew without a doubt that someone was going to hand the nursing administration her own head on a platter.

Maybe I'll just walk down to the car, drive away, and never come back, Denise thought wearily. At home she had an application for one of the most prestigious medical schools in the country. She could fill it out, go into medicine, and never have to deal with anything like this again. She'd be on the other side of the desk, working as a doctor, not a nurse.

The phone rang. It took Denise a moment to focus, then she picked up the receiver.

"Denise Frazier, please." The voice was male and deep, slightly threatening.

"Speaking."

"Ms. Frazier, are both Keith Jennings and Emily Greer on duty tonight?"

"Who is this?"

"Dr. Wankle."

Denise sighed and closed her eyes. Of course. Dr. Wankle was the director of medical administration—it made sense that he would be the one to call. No doubt he had the *Mercury* in front of him, and had zeroed in on the names mentioned in the story. It wouldn't take much detective work for him to realize that Emily was the nurse referred to in the final paragraph.

"I will be at the hospital in forty-five minutes. I expect to see all three of you in the conference room, third floor. Be there."

Denise hung up the phone. *Be there*. He was the top man, he was important, so anything having to do with the day-to-day care of patients was beneath his notice. The fact that he would be taking away half of the work team on Ridge Six East was of no consequence.

"You look like a truck just ran over you." Terry Barnall stood at the desk, looking over the records for a new patient who had just been admitted to Neurosurgical Care.

"I didn't get the license number," Denise sighed. "Have you seen this article?"

Terry shook his head and took the proffered paper. It took him about thirty seconds to read it.

"And that phone call was probably from Wankle or whoever's just below him, right? He wants to see you?"

"And Keith and Emily," Denise said.

"Would you mind if I come along? I know quite a bit about what happened with Emily's daughter, Colleen. Wankle might be interested to discover what else has been going on around here."

Denise looked up at him with new hope. She hadn't even dreamed that a doctor, particularly one who had something to lose, might be willing to confront the hospital administration.

Within forty-five minutes, Emily, Keith, Terry, and Denise were awaiting the arrival of the eminent Dr. Wankle. They didn't have to wait long.

"What the hell *is* this? What kind of irresponsible idiots do we have working for us, that you, *any* of you, would take it upon yourselves to tell a newspaper about our internal problems? Why didn't you come to me? Why wasn't this brought to the attention of the administration? Did you think of that? No, you had to spread our dirty laundry outside, where everyone can see it!" Wankle was shouting, his wizened, raisinlike face almost purple with fury. His white hair, usually carefully coifed, stood on end as he repeatedly ran his hands through it.

"Dr. Wankle . . . " Denise began.

"Shut up, damn it! I don't want any of your lame excuses."

"Dr. Wankle, this is *not* an excuse, and you may not talk to me in that way. I don't care what your position is in this hospital—you are obliged to treat us with the same courtesy you would show any of your colleagues," Denise said icily.

Terry looked over at her and hid a smile. So this was the role model for the other nurses on the sixth floor. Denise was one-hundred-percent professional and she wasn't going to allow anyone, doctor or patient, to forget it.

"I'll have the lot of you dismissed!" It was obvious that the doctor was not only tired—he was frantic with worry. He'd almost reached retirement age and he had to stop the damage before it affected him. But there was the thought, deeply hidden, that disaster had already reached him if this newspaper story had even a shred of truth in it. Wankle would be retired before he wanted to go, under a cloud, his reputation tarnished. It was Wankle's private opinion that all those damn people of color should be sent right over to County to begin with.

Wankle put his hands to his head, mussing his hair even more as he tried to make sense of what was happening to him and to Ridge.

"You'll have us dismissed? On what grounds?" Emily spoke up.

"On the grounds that your continued presence here is inimical to the continued well-being of Ridge Hospital!"

Emily gritted her teeth, determined not to let this man cow her into submission. "Dr. Wankle, maybe you'll reconsider your protestations that *we* caused damage when you learn that two physicians here at Ridge tried to kill my daughter," she said quietly.

"Don't give me any of that idiotic twaddle! You don't know what you're talking about."

Terry decided it was time to step in. "Dr. Wankle, we've met previously. I am Terry Barnall, chief resident, neurosurgery." Terry waited for Wankle to acknowledge his presence.

"Yes, Doctor? I cannot imagine what you're doing here. I specifically asked for only those people named or referred to in that scurrilous article."

"I'm here because I was directly involved in the case of Mrs. Greer's daughter. I was very much aware of the punitive actions taken by those two doctors toward Colleen Greer. It was clearly a matter of retaliation against the child's mother for refusing to accept responsibility for the patient who blew himself up, smoking while he was on oxygen."

Wankle frowned. He remembered the case perfectly well. He'd thought then that Emily Greer, the nurse who let it happen, should have been shot on the spot. He smiled slowly. It wasn't a nice smile.

"I don't believe you've been notified yet, Mrs. Greer, but there is still a formal complaint pending about your actions. Dr. O'Shea is no longer able to press charges, but in light of the newspaper article, we will definitely proceed to meet with the Nursing Administration."

"Frankly, sir, I don't care what you do," Emily told him. "I will be delighted to tell my side of that story again, and then I will tender my resignation from this hospital. But it will be my decision, not one I was forced into by your anger."

Keith stepped forward. "And as for me, you already have my resignation on the desk. I've found a much better job. Ridge won't miss me, and I'm not going to miss Ridge." He turned and marched from the room. There was no reason to stay around any longer. Besides, he wanted to get to a phone and tell Bill Sonderson about Dr. Wankle's meeting. It would do him a world of good to know that his initial article had already precipitated a shakeup in the hospital administration. He knew a desperate man when he saw one—Dr. Wankle was definitely in trouble.

Dr. Wankle looked at the closed door and passed his hand over his face. So he didn't have to worry about that male nurse. Good. Now all he had to do was get rid of the doctor and the other two nurses.

"Mrs. Greer, do you actually expect me to believe that physicians on our staff attempted to harm your daughter as retaliatory action against you?" Wankle blustered.

The sound of Terry's beeper cut through Dr. Wankle's question. He saw the red message flash— another emergency, call 211-03 immediately. He didn't wait for Wankle to say anything more. He had never knuckled under to pressure and he wasn't about to start now. And Emily wasn't fair game, either.

"Dr. Wankle, I believe Emily has already answered that. And you have no reason to question Denise. May I suggest that you go home and allow us all to get back to work?" Terry stated it as a request, but one that would be difficult to ignore.

"But I have more questions . . . " Wankle thundered.

"If you do, sir, then I suggest you question us in front of witnesses, with the Nursing Administration and the hospital attorney present," Denise put in.

"I will not!"

Terry, Denise, and Emily looked at each other. Simultaneously all of them turned and walked out the door, leaving Wankle sputtering threats behind them.

"Emily, wait a minute." Terry held her back so Denise could go on ahead of them down the corridor.

"Are you still interested in breakfast? This whole mess didn't scuttle our plans, did it?"

"Of course not. I'll be ready and waiting."

Terry's beeper started again, and he shrugged apologetically. "Later, Emily." And he was gone, charging down the stairs because the elevator would have taken forever.

Emily didn't have time to think about Terry or anything but her patients during the rest of her shift. There were still eight hours' work to do when she came back. The few nurses who had been left with the whole section had handed out meds, but that was all. Nothing else had been done. There were patient records to be updated, medications to be ordered, and rounds to be made.

Emily did, however, make time to stop in and see Leopold Peters, even though he wasn't her patient for the night. Peters was reading when she came into the room. He looked up, scowled, and threw the magazine down on the bed.

"Damn it, I just got poked, prodded, and listened to! Are you going to do it again?" he asked testily. Emily could tell that he was feeling better. His color was good, he was moving easily in the bed, and being his usual obnoxious self.

"No, Mr. Peters, I am not here to poke or prod. I came to say thank you. I got the check and all the papers today. I know you had to work from your hospital bed to get the matter taken care of, and I just wanted to say how much I appreciate it."

Peters looked uncomfortable. He wasn't very good at accepting thanks. He went out of his way to be a curmudgeon, and the more people who accepted him at face value, the better.

"I only did it because you're a good nurse, and because I hate to see someone act toward his own kid

227

the way Nicholas did toward Colleen. So don't start saying I'm a nice guy. If you hadn't been a solid, good, efficient nurse, even with an old bastard like me, you'd never have seen a penny of that money without going back to court. Now get out of here— you've got other patients to take care of."

He grabbed the magazine and hid behind it, pretending to be engrossed in an article about *amicus curiae* briefs.

Emily smiled, remembering her murderous intentions on more than one occasion. Then she left the room, closing the door behind her.

The shift finally ended, and Emily stood in the lobby, waiting for Terry. Her hopes were rising again, despite her best intentions of simply allowing whatever happened to happen. She wouldn't let herself get any romantic ideas—they'd only be dashed.

"Emily, how much time do you have before you need to pick up Colleen and take her to school?" Terry looked frazzled. He had on a clean, crisp white coat, but everything else was wrinkled, including his tie.

"About forty-five minutes. Why?" Emily said. Her heart was beginning to sink again.

He sighed. "Then can I take a rain check until this afternoon? I'm going to go up and grab some orange juice and get back down to Peds. They've got a shunt going bad, and I'm the only one who has any experience with it." Terry looked desperately unhappy. He looked, Emily thought, the way she felt. Damn it, she'd allowed her wishes to take over again, and it hurt.

Terry saw her face and shook his head. "Emily, it's not that I don't want to be with you. Oh, hell, I was going to wait until we were alone, and I could do this in privacy and with a romantic atmosphere and all that, but . . ." He reached into his pocket, brought out a small, red velvet box, and offered it to her.

Emily took it, hardly daring to believe her eyes. No, of course it couldn't be . . .

"I'm afraid I don't have time for romance and all the trappings right now. But the time we've spent together has been wonderful, even when Colleen was sick. I want to marry you, and if I don't ask you right now, I may never get up the courage again. . . . Damn it!" Terry heard the shrilling of his beeper and cut the sound off abruptly. He didn't even look down to see the message.

Emily flipped open the box and took out the diamond ring with a hand that trembled. It wasn't as big as the one Nicholas had given her, but it was lovely, with graceful arcs of gold, and the small stone set bravely in the middle.

"I can get you a bigger one later . . . " Terry said hopefully. For just a minute he looked like a small boy, afraid that his offering wouldn't be good enough.

"Oh, Terry, it's beautiful," Emily breathed. "And you want to marry me? You really do?" She couldn't help it—she was going to cry, she knew she was.

"I love you, Emily. I want to marry you and stay with you forever and make little brothers and sisters for Colleen—whenever we both have the time," Terry said. He kissed her then, and they were both blissfully unaware of the other people who were passing by and smiling at the scene.

"I'd love to marry you," Emily said quietly when her lips were free. Imagine, she thought, how happy Nicholas would be—he wouldn't have to pay alimony anymore! She giggled at the irrelevance of the idea.

Terry's beeper shrilled again, angry, insistent, calling him back to his patients.

"It'll always be like this. But never forget for one instant that I love you!" Terry said. He kissed her lightly one more time and dashed out of the lobby. Emily gazed after him, pressing the ring against her cheek.

"I love you, too, Dr. Barnall," she whispered. "But if we ever have a honeymoon, you're leaving that beeper at home!"

In Book Three of the R.N. series . . .

When Vickie Pearson is admitted to Ridge Hospital for tests to determine the source of her recurrent chest pains, her presence immediately causes quite a stir. Vickie's claim to be psychic fascinates some patients and members of the staff while antagonizing others. She's been assigned to nurse Cathy Wescott, but Cathy asks charge nurse Denise Frazier to take her off the case, confiding to Denise that Vickie makes her very uncomfortable—occult mumbo-jumbo has no place in a modern, efficient hospital.

Denise obliges by giving Vickie's case to Julie Phillips, and the two women become good friends. Julie's insecurities and worries about her competence as a nurse begin to abate with Vickie's help and advice. And she's intrigued when Vickie reads the cards and indicates that there is a major change approaching in Julie's future.

But Julie's positive attitude is not shared by Dr. Matt Harper, who resents what he terms Vickie's "interference" in the lives of patients and staff alike, and Cathy backs him up. Meanwhile, Cathy's personal life is becoming increasingly stressful. Her husband wants to move halfway across the country to Vermont and take over his grandfather's farm, but Cathy hates the idea of leaving Chicago and the excitement of her nursing career in a big city hospital. Though Vickie offers her help, Cathy shies away from her—until a series of incidents begins to convince her that there may be more to Vickie's powers than she had previously believed. . . .

Watch for

Visions

next in the *R.N.* series
from Lynx Books!